A Silent Pain

Nara Somaratne

'The way you torture your husband is far more
worse than what our mother did to our father.'

An angry brother's stern warning to his younger sister
in 1986 at his residence in Warradale, Adelaide.

Publisher: Inspiring Publishers,
P.O. Box 159, Calwell, ACT Australia 2905
Email: publishaspg@gmail.com
http://www.inspiringpublishers.com

 A catalogue record for this book is available from the National Library of Australia

National Library of Australia The Prepublication Data Service

Author: Nara Somaratne
Title: A Silent Pain
Genre: Fiction

Paperback ISBN: 978-1-923087-49-1

Preface

A general belief in society regarding domestic violence is that women are typically the victim with the perpetrator generally being a husband, ex-husband or partner. Yet according to the literature, the startling truth is that one-third of domestic abuse victims are men. Men tend to hide this from the external world due to pervading attitudes in society around masculinity, an individual's personality and social status, and the hostility that may be encountered if they do open up. Therefore, the actual number may be higher than reported. In contrast, the public consciousness tends to associate domestic violence, either physical or verbal violence, by a man against a woman with whom he is an intimate relationship. Women have powerful tools to use, such as sympathy, femininity, and tears. The purpose of this work is to convey to people that both men and women who have suffered from domestic violence *can* survive and move on with their lives and reach happiness. It also advocates the following:

- If you are contemplating suicide, talk to a close friend.
- If you are in love with someone, do not marry anyone else.
- If you have a duty, do it, no matter how many difficulties you may face.
- Forget the past and stay with your own consciousness. You can find happiness, which is not too far away; it is within you.

Nara Somaratne

Meaning of Sinhala words in this book

Achchi, Appachchi: Father

Amma: Mother

Aiya: Elder brother

Akka: Elder sister

Bappa: Father's younger brother

Chena: Shifting agricultural practice by clearing of forest land

Duwa: Daughter

Kachcheri: Government's District Administrative Office

Loku Amma: Mother's elder sister

Loku Appachchi: Father's elder brother

Lokuputha: Elder son

Loku Mahaththaya: Head master of the school

Mama, Mamandi: Mother's brother, or uncle

Malli: Younger brother

Miniha: Impolite way to call a man or husband

Mudalali: Businessman

Nandamma: Father's sister

Nangi: Younger sister

Punchi Amma: Mother's younger sister, or wife of *Bappa*

Roti: Flat bread

Saree: Principal outer garment of women in Indian subcontinent

Sarong: Large tube or length of fabric wrap around the waist

Veddah: Sri Lankan aboriginal who used to live in the forest

Wedamahaththaya: Village Ayurvedic physician

Chapter 1

The Attempt

It was the morning of 12th January 2019. It took nearly two hours to write the letter to the police and coroner with a trembling hand. It was not an easy decision to end my life, but there was no other way to relieve the pain. There was nobody in this world for me, no one cared about me, no one talked to me. I had no one near and dear to me to talk to. I couldn't even think of anything else. Since I made the decision to end my life that morning, my whole body started to tremble like a fish out of water. My shirt was wet with sweat and my breathing was short and shallow. My head was heavy and the pain in my chest was unbearable, but I kept writing another short letter to my children which simply said: 'I love you all, *Achchi*.'

Knowing that this was my last day alive brought back lots of memories, randomly crossing my mind one after the other. There were thousands of stories I could have written but I ended up writing only one line for my children. I could not say what was truly on my mind – that continuing to live my life seemed no longer meaningful since my marriage of 35 years had ended, leaving me with nothing. The crushing, unbearable weight of my thoughts meant that I needed to end my life to permanently find calm and give me peace. There was no other solution.

I had been born and raised in a family of eight siblings, and during the course of my life, through study and work had made lots of friends. However, there I was that day alone, no family members to talk to despite having three grown-up children. My daughter had left to stay with her mother; my elder son had married and was living in a distant suburb with his family; and my younger son had moved to Melbourne, even though he was here for the Christmas holiday and had stayed with me in the family home in Wattle Park, an upmarket Adelaide suburb. He had left for Melbourne a few days before, in the first week of January and I was all alone in the house.

I was imprisoned in my own home. My mind was jumping between thoughts of my brother and sisters, children and grandchildren, friends and colleagues and thoughts of loneliness were pushing me to the edge. It was almost like the Sinhalese stage-play *Sinhabahu* and how the lion wept in anger and frustration as his wife and children left him. As the chorus of the play goes: "The love for children has penetrated the skin, muscles and veins; gone up to the bones and entered the bones, and rests on the bone marrow bringing eternal pain." I was experiencing the same thing as the lion did in that play.

I couldn't eat or drink, sleep or go out, and the feeling of isolation was hurting deeply inside and causing a heaviness in my head and chest. The sudden loss of my family, without even a slight warning, was intolerable, relentlessly causing pain.

I had started to blame and condemn myself for becoming angry with my wife. I felt worthless, ashamed, guilty, humiliated and rejected by my own family. I had no contact with my siblings and their children in Sri Lanka, no close friends around except some school friends and batch-mates from college who lived interstate, and no hope for the future. The ceaseless flow of thoughts from a happier past to this present misery made it difficult to think about any kind of future. Thoughts crossed my mind about my family in Sri Lanka as I had not seen some of them for several years, but I did not have any contact details for them. The only thing I could do was walk between rooms – hundreds of times into my daughter's room but she was there no more. I look at photos of my family, but no one was around. No one was in the kitchen. There was no daughter in the kitchen baking my favorite lamington cake. The television had been silent for several days. I sat on the verandah in a folding chair for several hours just looking at the horizon beyond Adelaide city.

In the evening, I decided to swallow one month of medication in one go. If I did that here in my home, nobody would know that I was decaying, and it would become a deceased estate so the house couldn't be sold as planned. Instead, I packed the medication and a bottle of water to take to the park on the Parade. I shaved and had a shower and ate some left-over rice and lentil curry that my younger son had cooked while he was still at home. By this time, the fear factor had gone, and I dressed in clean clothes and sat on the couch to wait until dark, usually around 8:30 pm. The following morning, the body would be found there in a public place.

I felt a pain in my neck and realised I was dressed like I was going to work. I checked the time, and it was after 4:30 am on Sunday morning. I realised what had happened. I was supposed to go to the park to commit suicide, but I had fallen asleep and accidentally missed the event. The heaviness in my head has gone, and I felt a little more relaxed. A second thought crossed my mind, and I decided not to go ahead with the suicide. I changed my clothes and decided in the morning I would call some friends who lived in Brisbane.

The first person I called was Justin, a school friend and batch-mate. I told him everything that had happened. We talked for a long time, and he told me never to think of suicide and that this idea had come about because my mind was disturbed. He suggested I start to meditate to quiet the mind. It seemed he meditated twice a day, morning and evening and had been practising for a long time.

Next I called Sarath, a long-time friend and manager from when I was working in Sri Lanka. He said something similar to what Justin had said, and suggested this kind of thinking had come about because I had abandoned my religious practices. He mentioned that a highly educated and respected monk from Sri Lanka was visiting Australia and would be in the Adelaide temple the following week conducting meditation sessions.

The next day when I went to work, my concentration was poor and I had difficulty focusing. I told my manager and friend Glenn that I intended to resign and I submitted my resignation with one month's notice. I also applied for one week's leave to attend sermons and meditation sessions given by the Sri Lankan Buddhist priest in the temple. Glenn asked what I intended to do, and I told him I was planning to return to Sri Lanka to live in a home for elders, and that I had no interest in being in Adelaide anymore, since I didn't know anyone. My family was now broken, and they had left me alone.

One day when daughter came to see me, I told her my plans. I had searched for somewhere to go in Sri Lanka and found a home for elders in Horana. I had never been to Horana before, and it would be a new environment. I told my daughter I was planning to give her my share of the house, and she seemed happy. She asked me to send details as to where I would be living when I got settled in Sri Lanka so they could come and visit. She didn't utter a word about me staying here and that they would be there for me. Nothing at all.

However, my decision to go to Sri Lanka was reversed after a lunch at the Adelaide Central Market with Jeff from Mount Gambier and some other colleagues. They commented on how it could be uncomfortable for me to live in Sri Lanka with ongoing medical conditions. After all, in Australia no one goes hungry and there is always help available. Jeff suggested there were a number of retirement villages in Mount Gambier I might like to check out, and I could buy an independent unit and stay there. He said he would be there for me when needed. I discussed it later with Glenn, and he agreed that was a good idea, but suggested I find somewhere nearby and that way I could withdraw my resignation and continue to work.

> *If you are on the edge of the abyss, don't jump.*
> *If you are going through hell, don't stop.*
> *As long as you are breathing, there is hope.*
> *As long as day follows night, there is hope.*
> *Nothing stays the same forever.*
> *Set an intention to heal, reach out for support and*
> *you will find help.*
>
> *Douglas Bloch, Healing from Depression*

Chapter 2

Childhood struggle
and the road to Success

It was close to midnight when someone woke me up – either *Amma* or Yakalla *Akka*. All four of the younger siblings were sleeping laid out on the floor in a row, lazily snuggled up on the mat together. Often my younger sisters would sleep closest to mother, though we each would take a turn. I was still half asleep even after repeated attempts to wake me. I would sit up and then fall back on the mat, but my elder sister, Yakalla *Akka,* kept us moving. She told us to wash our faces and get dressed to go to our ancestral village.

'We're going to our village?' I asked.

'Yes, we have to go and see *Appachchi* as he is sick,' she said.

We all rushed to clean our teeth with Gopal tooth powder and wash our faces. 'Getting dressed' simply meant wearing the sarong I was already in and adding a shirt I normally wore to school. There were two cars parked in front of the house. I heard my brother say the cars belonged to our uncle *Bappa*, the younger brother of my father. One of the drivers was Jaya *Aiya*, my father's elder brother's son, and the other person I cannot identify. I had seen Jaya *Aiya* before when I had been to our ancestral village, Kannehepola – once with my father in a hired car and once with my mother in a bus. Both Jaya *Aiya* and the other person were talking to our neighbours in low voices. The neighbours were Samithin, Siriya, the carpenter George Botheju and Mahatthaya *Mamandi* of the Amunugama house, located just opposite our house. They talked in low voices and we couldn't hear what they were saying but mother might have guessed something was wrong with my father. Jaya *Aiya* apparently told her my father was sick and wanted to see the family. Mother had dressed in one of her two *sarrees* and was wearing her one and only pair of silver bangles. Yakalla *Akka* wore a *redda* (half sarree) and a jacket, and my brother, like me, was wearing a sarong and a shirt. Our two younger sisters, Seela and Kumari, wore gowns.

On the way, we might have slept in the car because the next thing I knew was the car was parked in front of a bungalow type large house. There were several people in the front yard, though it was close to dawn, and the front yard and house were lighted with large lamps. We all jumped out of the cars and as we went into the house, I could hear my mother crying. As we entered everyone in the house started to cry and we were guided to the front room of the house.

There he was, my father, laid out in a beautiful coffin, dressed in white lace cloth and with white-gloves on his hands which were on his chest, his eyes closed. We all started to cry along with my mother. Kanumale *Nandamma* was sitting there crying when we arrived and mother asked her what had happened. With tears, she explained, my father was bitten by a pet dog in a nearby house. It was only later that the dog showed signs of hydrophobia (rabies), and by the time father was admitted to the Kurunegala hospital, it was too late to be treated. He died a few days later.

The funeral was attended by a large number of people, as father's younger brother was a significant businessman, so almost all our relatives and the rest of the villagers were there. One special person there was Reverend Weragoda, vicar of Kurunegala, where my elder sister, Sudu *Akka* was working as a domestic servant. Father was burried on the land that once belonged to him, where his family home was before he had left for Huruluwewa. At the time of his burial, it belonged to his younger brother, as my father had sold the place to him. We stayed in Kanumale *Nandamma*'s house and visited other relatives frequently. After the seventh day of alms giving, we stayed around another two to three weeks before heading back to Huruluwewa.

During this time, my brother and I explored the fields, the nearby water course (Maguru Oya) and walked through coconut plantations picking various fruits and berries as well as watching large monitor lizards. We bathed in Maguru Oya, and one day we saw a village woman come in. She took our soap bar and started to wash-and-clean her bundle of clothes. My brother went to take our soap back and the woman bit his palm. We ran home and told everyone, and *Mamandi*, mother's elder brother, told everyone he had heard there was a mad-woman roaming around the area and to take care of ourselves.

We fell in love with our village – it was far lovelier than the barren lands where we lived in Huruluwewa. My elder sisters showed us a large number of coconut plantations and a rice field that our father once owned. He might have been rich at that time in the 1950s. Just before we were to leave, several relatives asked my mother to leave my brother and I with them so they could educate us and to take the girls with her. This was no merciful help, as the real intention was to keep the boys for working in their fields and to do all the farming jobs. Thankfully, my mother realised what they were up to and took *all* her children with her to Huruluwewa, where we had no close relatives or friends, except the settlers we had come to know over the last eight years. The burden on my mother's shoulders must have been unbearably tremendous, as she had no fixed income and no grown-up male sons to work in the paddy fields or on the land at the time.

We took a bus from Kurunegala to Kekirawa via Kalawewa. I always enjoyed this trip and kept watching how the landscape changed from Kurunegala to Kekirawa. It was a drought year, 1961, and the Kalawewa water level was very low. People were catching small fish using small cane baskets and spreading them on the slope of the tank bund for drying. From Kekirawa, mother bought some vegetables and rice to cook for dinner. Punchi *Amma*, Kanumale *Nandamma* and other relatives must have given her some money for the trip back and living expenses for a couple of months. When we arrived home, we heard the news that our house was about to be occupied by a relative of the Amunugama house, as everyone had thought after my father's death no one would ever return.

It was several years earlier, probably 1956, when my father took me to the local school, Padikaramaduwa Vidyalaya, and enrolled me there. The school comprised two identical buildings – one for the school itself and the other for rice storage during harvesting time since the number of students at the school was low enough that both buildings were not needed. The school building consisted of just one long hall, not separate classrooms. At one end, there was a stage where the headmaster (*Loku Mahaththaya*), Mr MK Sirisena's office was. From there, he could see the entire school so everyone was on their best behaviour, both students and teachers. Father gave me a bundle of beetle leaves and asked me to give it to the *Loku Mahaththaya*. I knelt down, prostrated in a typical Sri Lankan manner. He raised me up, took me by his side and started to read me the Sinhala albhabet and a few words. After this, he patted me on my head and asked me to study well at his school and sent me to the classroom.

This was the beginning of my education. In preparatory classes and class 1, the class-teachers were mostly ladies. One of them was AG Siriyawathie (*Loku Nona Mahaththaya*), the headmaster's very kind wife. They lived in the school bungalow located next to the school building.

For the first year or two, school life went smoothly except for one male teacher whose name was also Sirisena. He always walked with a cane in his hand. Whenever I saw him, I was overcome with fear and started weeing in my clothes. Punchi *Akka* would come and take me to the nearby Huruluwewa right-bank main canal to wash me and dry my clothes. After this, she took me back to the classroom. Unfortunately, this interrupted her school education, as she missed many classes because of me. On rainy days, father would come to take us home, with banana leaves as umbrellas. Many houses, including ours, did not have umbrellas and most of the time we used either a banana leave or a gunny bag to cover our heads. Sometimes father used to put me on his shoulders and carry me home.

A significant change to my education began when Mr Samarakoon became class 2 teacher. He was from the neighouring Nikawewa colony. Under his guidance, I became the top student in my class, maintaining this position throughout my education until I left the school in 1966 at the end of class 9 and securing first place every term and in the end-of-year tests.

One day when Mr Samarakoon saw that I was wearing a shirt with stitches all over it, he bought me a new shirt and asked me to wear it to school. There was no particular school uniform at the time, just a sarong and shirt, or shorts and shirt. Girls wore gowns. Almost everyone came to school barefoot, typical of the children of poor families.

I had several friends at school. Each of the colonies identified from which district the majority of people came from. Close to the Huruluwewa tank was the Nuwara Eliya colony, then Rambawewa and Aba colonies. We lived in Kurunegala colony with the majority from Kurunegala district, and sometimes from neighbouring villages. My friends were from different colonies: Rajamanthree and Dinadasa were from Nuwara Eliya colony; Gunarath Banda and Ranbanda (Bandirala's sons), Jayalath, two Abeyratanes; Karunaratne, Ariyaratne and Pemaratne (*Balla Gedara*-house with a dog) were from our area; Gunaratne was from *Aba*-colony and Piyadasa from Rambawewa colony. People from each colony spoke Sinhala with minor dialects, and so did the children. It was bit funny since each other come from different colonies. In the latter part of class 3, I had two special friends, Nimal and Wimal, who were the headmaster's sons. (These two became close friends and our friendship ran into adulthood.) This was bit unusual as they were not allowed to move with every student in their classes. Their parents were worried they might pick up some bad habits from children of colonists. I was quite a shy student and good at my studies, so I was allowed to be friends with them.

At home I had three friends, my brother and two younger sisters Seela and Kumari, and also our uncle Appuhamy's children until they were resettled in newly established Rajangana colony in mid-1960. There were several changes happening on the home front. Sudu *Akka* became very sick frequently, as she could not tolerate the dusty, warm weather that prevailed most of the year. Father took her back to the ancestral village, and she stayed at Kanumale *Nandamma*'s place. From there, she moved to the Kurunegala vicar's house as a domestic servant. Punchi *Akka* was also taken away and became a domestic servant for a business family that lived on Wilgoda Road.

Father had started to sell his remaining lands one by one, and each time he did, he bought lorry-loads of goods for sale. Once he bought clay pots, as most of the villagers did not have enough (new settlers had brought only a couple of cooking pots with them); another time he bought banana and coconut plants. Being a good farmer, he planted coconut, jack fruit, cadju nut trees and banana plants on our land of 1.5 acres. But he was not a good businessman nor did he have any skills in selling goods, so most of the plants and clay pots he bought, he ended up giving away to people who asked for them. One time, after selling some land, he bought a bullock-cart with two black bulls, only to sell them again a few months later. My brother and I watched the cart being taken away by the new owner with tears in our eyes. During rainy season, when paddy fields were prepared for cultivation, father took us to the paddy field. In those days, there were only a few tractors there to plough, so most of the time rice bays had to be prepared using buffalos for puddling. People had to prepare bunds of rice bays to store water. We were involved in all the activities, as it was a learning process for us as well as providing lots of fun.

Father had the habits of drinking and swallowing opium three or four times a day. Most of the money he earned from working and selling his lands was spent mainly on opium. He would go to Kurunegala to buy opium, and when he come home, other opium users such as Rapiel (equivalent of Rafael) who lived two houses away came and borrowed from him, never to pay him yet again. As father was bold, he was nick-named Oliver (after Sir Oliver Goonetilleke, the Governor General at the time who was also a bold person), and his friends would call me Oliver's son or Oliver *Aiya*'s son.

From childhood I had a good reading habit but there were no extra reading materials available, so I read every little piece of paper that came wrapped around sugar, salt and other groceries. As I grew up, I walked to the boutique shop to read the daily newspapers, mainly *Dinamina* and *Lankadeepa*. Sometimes, old people who were illiterate or had weak eyesight asked me to read aloud to them.

When my father died in 1961, any connection to our ancestral village was lost, except for the occasional visit from my mother on her way to Inguruwatte. I usually went with her and sometimes my two younger sisters came as well. Occasionally, my eldest sister, Inguruwatte *Akka* would visit us, sometimes her husband Inguruwatte *Aiya* alone. There was no other visitor, either from paternal or maternal sides.

No matter how poor and helpless, we were well-protected and taken care of. We were not allowed to move with mischievous children around the neighbourhood. We always followed what mother or our elder sisters said to us. Once, my brother and I went fishing with some other boys who would regularly go to catch fish. It was a common practice for boys to go fishing during the season when water was issued in the main canal. We did not have hooks, so we secretly made them with safety pins and borrowed strings from a friend. Following what the other boys did, we used earth worms as bait. Both of us caught some fish and tied it to a thread and carried it home. We had one big worry though – would our elder sister throw them away and punish us? As we approached the house hesitantly, we saw at a distance that Yakalla *Akka* was in front of the house. We kept walking slowly, fearfully, as we approached the house, ready to run away if she started to scold us. To our surprise, she was smiling and asked us to give her the fish to clean. Thinking that we may have a freshly caught fish curry for dinner, we handed them over, and as we did, she caught both of us and took us to a nearby papaya tree, tied us to it and hit us with a stick. This was my first and last animal kill. We later found out she apparently knew we were fishing and had planned her strategy ahead of us coming home with our catch.

Around 1962, Yakalla *Akka* got married to RM Ranhamy, who was from Illuppukanniya, along the road from Yakalla to Anuradhapura. At the time, he was working for the Land Development Department as a labourer and had been working in the area. He had rented a place and neighbours had proposed the marriage. It was a simple wedding – only family members and few neighbours attended. Ranhamy *Aiya* was an active person and good at farming. After they were married, he came to live with us and started to build an additional two rooms and a kitchen. A few months later Yakalla *Akka* went to Kokawewa with her husband, about 15 kilometres away at the end of Huruluwewa right-bank main canal, since Ranhamy *Aiya* was working in the area at the time.

During school holidays, I spent time in Illuppukanniya and on another occasion at Kokawewa. During particularly dry years, water was scarce for bathing, so we would walk several kilometres to either Huruluwewa or to wells dug in drainage canals in rice fields. There were no crops grown; even perennial plants such as banana and coconut trees could not survive. As a drought relief provision, the Government found work for people repairing irrigation canals and local roads, which involved excavation of soil and filling potholes or repairing bunds. It was extremely difficult to dig in clay-rich soils that were compacted. Even for young males, it was hard to achieve daily targets. A supervisor measured the earth work and accordingly provided a ration card for buying food stuff, usually wheat flour.

At times, young men from the neighbourhood kindly helped my mother with excavating. Other times, to survive, she took work as a labourer in a metal quarry and on chilli and tobacco farms for a daily wage of 3 rupees. It was hard going, and sometimes mother relied on a small amount of money – most likely around 20 rupees at a time – sent by Suddu *Akka*. At other times, she helped grind *kurakkan* (millet) or dehusk rice at other people's houses. When eggplants were freely available in abandoned *chena* (a shifting agricultural practice involving rotation of crops and not using the same piece of land), mother and my elder sisters would pick them, cook them in a large pot and we would eat them with a little piece of *roti* bread. There were days, we had only boiled pumpkin or green papaya for dinner. Mother always ate last, eating the leftovers after feeding her children. She kept this practice until her final days, always serving herself last. I saw tears in her eyes at times, as she told the story of the hardships and burden of raising children without an adult male in the family.

After several years of drought, in 1963, the rains came and people were given loans to buy seed, and ploughing and land preparation for *Yala* season began (May–August: northeast monsoon). All the people had to go to the nearest town, Galenbindunuwewa to collect their loans as the government officials only came there because of its central location. I went with my mother and stood in a queue until our turn came. Those who got their money counted and moved away. When my mother's turn came, she went to the desk and, being unable to write, she applied ink to her thumb and make a thrumb print. The person on the desk told her to go away and come back with her *miniha* (impolite word for husband) otherwise they wouldn't give her the money. Mother moved away helplessly, with tears, as there was no one there to help her. I was her only sympathiser, until one kind officer noticed her tears and called her over. Softly, he told her to bring a letter from *Gramasewaka* (a government officer) or the death certificate, then they would consider giving her the loan on a later date.

Those people who got their loans were full of joy, talking and laughing, and since it was close to Sinhala new year festival, they all went shopping. They bought plenty of grocery items; almost everyone bought a large dry fish – a delicacy in Sri Lanka. Some bought kettles and some even bought bottles of arrack to celebrate. Others, accompanied by their spouses, bought clothes for the new year. It seemed everyone had forgotten, probably deliberately, that the loan was meant for preparing paddy fields and buying seeds.

The trip home was equally painful. We were walking behind people who lived close to our house: Mohotha, Aruma, Peruma, Pubilis Sinho, Punchinaide. Some of them were laughing and sarcastically said to my mother: 'You didn't get the loan, how are you going to celebrate the new year?' Mother didn't utter a word, just kept walking with me by her side. I now feel how much pain she must have gone through.

Eventually, she was able to get the loan just as the season was about to start. Someone surely must have helped her prepare the documents. She bought rice seeds, and paid Banda for the ploughing, since he was the only person who owned a tractor. He was from Rambawewa and was known locally as a rich man. Even though the required fee was paid in advance, Banda never ploughed our field as 'no adult' male was at home and it was not a priority for him. This was quite evident in all circumstances, and mother had to go to his place and pleaded for him to plough our field. In the end, he did, but at the very end of the season, when most of the other fields' rice had germinated. The ploughing was also not done properly; Banda just moved the tractor here and there, leaving large unploughed patches everywhere in the field, so that lots of manual preparation was still required.

One day, my youngest sister, Kumari, came home after playing with the children of Punchinaide *Wedamahaththaya*, the local traditional Ayurvedic doctor. She asked mother, 'Don't we have any relatives?' Everyone was surprised why all of a sudden little Kumari would ask this question. When mother replied that we did, in Kurunegala, Kumari asked why they didn't come and see us. Mother sat down on the floor, and tears started to flow down her cheeks, but she didn't reply. Kumari then explained she'd had a piece of pineapple at the house she had visited that day. Some relatives from Kurunegala were there, and they had brought pineapple with them. It was typical to bring pineapple or sweets such as cakes or sugar buns when relatives visited from ancestral villages. We never got them, except when Sudu *Akka* or Inguruwatte *Aiya* visited us. We never had many visitors, so no pineapple for Kumari.

Mother never spoke about our relatives or any other details of the livelihood that she had in the ancestral village. Mother never spoke about how our father sold the lands he owned and wasted the money. She never said a word of disrespect for my father. It is from our elder sisters that we came to know everything. She appeared, though uneducated, to accept the reality of life and face her destiny. She just kept quiet, only shedding tears when things became unbearable. This incident hit me hard, and I determined that someday I would take mother and all the family back to her village and settle there. I would try everything possible to get the glory we had lost. At the time I did not have any idea how to do it, but it has been the driving force behind me.

As any other child, we too liked sweets and other treats. There was a ritual practice in rural Sri Lanka to invoke the blessings of goddess *Paththini* onto expectant mothers, or mother and the child or even to a sick person. This is usually called *kiri amma dane* (alms giving for grandmothers). Whenever there was any *kiri amma dane* in the area, my mother was inevitably invited as she was a quiet and kind person. She lived up to the very meaning of the word 'mother.'

On the day, mother would get dressed in white clothes as she would to go to a temple, take a white towel with her and leave early in the morning. Usually, when an alms-giving ceremony is completed, *kevum* (oil cakes), *kiribath* (milk rice), kokis (a savoury) and other sweets are given to participating ladies to take home. We were anxiously waiting her return, Seela and Kumari by the gate.

After the rice fields were harvested, children would collect rice stalks left over in the fields as a way of earning some pocket money. Mature rice crops were harvested manually, kept on the ground to dry, and collected and bundled to carry for threshing. In this process, naturally some rice stalks were left in the fields. I used to go to the rice fields, sometimes alone and sometimes with my younger sisters. We would walk several kilometres searching for the stalks, which we would then bring home and thresh, and collect in small woven sacks. When we had collected sufficiently, our treasure was sold to buy pencils and exercise books, or lollies and sugar buns. It was satisfying earning.

Towards 1964, my mother went to Kurunegala and brought Punchi *Akka* home. With the arrival of Punchi *Akka*, our home front changed dramatically. It seemed like there were ten adult males in the house all of a sudden. She rounded us up and started clearing the land of 1.5 acres. During this period, growing tobacco and chilli was very attractive, and she started to grow these crops. We were given small plots of our own. I was very keen on agriculture and I had my own vegetable garden for home consumption.

With the onset of the rainy season, Punchi *Akka* started to plant manioc and work in the paddy field. Unlike other people, she never left bunds of rice bays without using them. She planted cowpea in all of them and they gave good harvest, and plenty for cooking. When in need, she gave some money to mother from her savings, every time saying, 'That is all I have.' When a small local handloom business started weaving clothes, particularly sarongs and blankets, towels and clothes that the village women wore, Punchi *Akka* started working there as a weaver. This brought a small amount of additional income, and we also got new sarongs. She was truly a brave young woman and a strict disciplinarian, never allowing her younger siblings to misbehave.

My favourite subject at school was geography. I was particularly interested in ancient civilisations and learning about other countries and cultures. In one of the books we studied in year 6 or 7, there was a section on Adelaide, Australia, where apples were grown and there were pictures of cold rooms where sheep carcasses were kept. I dreamed of one day seeing this place and other countries that I read about.

When I was in year 7 and 8, after school and on weekends, I would go to the school to study and do homework, as there was no desk and chair at home. Father had paid our neighbour, carpenter George Botheju, to make a full suite of furniture. He never completed it, except for a bed, an unfinished table and a chair. With the death of father, no one really cared for any furniture. Nimal and Wimal would join me to do their homework on weekends or after school. One weekend, after doing our homework, we were talking near the school bungalow and I heard the headmaster's wife talking to another lady teacher. She said that the driver Piyadasa had told her that those children (pointing to me) did not deserve to be living like this as they had had plenty in Kurunegala until their father sold everything.

In 1965, Nimal left the school to attend senior school in Kandy. I felt a deep sorrow as my best friend had moved away. Occasionally, we exchanged letters. I would await school holidays to see him and discuss various things; in particular I liked to hear about city school life, sports and other facilities there. By this time, Yakalla *Akka* had remarried, to PB Adassooriya, and gone to live with her husband in Yakalla – thus she became Yakalla *Akka*. Adassoriaya *Aiya* initially worked as a private car hire driver and then joined the Health Department as an ambulance driver. For a short period, he helped to run the shop owned by his elder sister's husband at Yakalla–Huruluwewa junction. They had a paddy field in the now-abandoned middle sluice gate canal of the Huruluwewa. I used to go to Yakalla during school holidays to help at the shop and also during the season to help in the paddy field. As I was very keen on agricultural activities and good at it too, the children of Yakalla *Akka* nicknamed me '*govirala mama*' (farming uncle).

One day in 1966, when I was in our rice field diverting water into rice bays, Samel's son who was in my class gave me the very exciting news that I had passed the year 8 scholarship and could go to Kekirawa Central College to study science stream subjects. The headmaster had announced this at the morning assembly. I was the only student in the area who passed the examination, and the only one to pursue secondary education in the science stream. On hearing the news, I came home to tell my mother, by which time she had already heard the news through my younger sisters and neighbours. It was the talking point of the people. At home, everyone was excited. Punchi *Akka*, who was sitting leaning against a wall, said, 'If this was a rich family, there would be lots of celebration today, but we don't have any money for that.' All talked about was how to find money to send me to the new school. We'd had a good tobacco harvest, and I had a separate area of cultivation of my own, so I thought I might sell my dried tobacco.

People around the neighbourhood, certainly other school children, looked at me with respect as if I had won the Nobel prize.

Some senior students told me what life might be like in the hostel, and that everything would be carried out according to a timetable. They said I would have to wear shoes, and attend sports and other co-curricular activities. All the paperwork to enrol at the central college had been done by the headmaster. Mother went to the DRO (Divisional Revenue Officer) office to get a letter stating that we were a low-income family. The scholarship covered food and accommodation in the school hostel up to university entrance.

The long-awaited letter arrived from the Kekirawa Central College, listing items that I had to bring with me into the hostel. A lockable trunk, white shorts and shirts as school uniforms, blue shorts and white vests for afternoon sports, black shoes to wear to school as part of the school uniform. Punchi *Akka* gave money to Adasooriya *Aiya*, and he went to Anuradhapura town and bought everything except shoes. On the day of admission, I went with Adasooriya *Aiya* to Kekirawa. We took the morning bus. At Kekirawa, he took me to a shoe shop and bought a pair of shoes. That was the first time I had worn shoes, and I was almost unable to walk in them. To me, it felt just like walking on the moon. I have never forgotten that experience; my feet were heavy and to take a step I had to lift my foot intentionally which made me unbalanced. Eventually I got used to it. For the admission, it seemed my mother's signature was required, so Adasooriya *Aiya* went back to Huruluwewa to bring my mother and around 4 pm I was admitted to the hostel.

There were several others from Anuradhapura and Polonnaruwa districts there. Just before tea-time, the hostel master introduced us to each other and to the prefects and hostel rules. We talked about our respective villages, the schools where we came from and about our parents' jobs. Most of the boys were from farming backgrounds, while some of their parents were teachers, village shop owners and public servants. Only one other boy, like me, did not have a father. His name was Kamalaratne and he later became my closest friend. He went on to Peradeniya University and became the school's physics teacher and principal. Naturally, we were the poorest of the poor. Kamalaratne also came to school with his mother and elder sister, who was just like my Punchi *Akka*, playing a similar role at home.

We newly arrived 'science scholars' were placed in year 9 science class, as we would have been in year 9 classes in our former village schools. The subjects we studied were foreign to us – physics, chemistry, mathematics, biology – and we struggled to understand. None of us had seen laboratory equipment such as beakers, thermometers or test tubes since we came from rural schools that had no such equipment. So the school then placed us in year 8, so we could get familiarised with mathematics and science subjects through studying general science first. I was not excelling in the class as there were several other brilliant students there, but managed to maintain top five.

I participated in almost every sports and athletic event but was not good at them. I joined the school's scouts and cadets as co-curricular activities. I was good at that and went on training to Diyathalawa army camp on three ocasions. These life experiences helped me build my character, determination, and ability to achieve results. Still, my purpose was to study well and get employed to look after my mother and help my siblings and their children.

These were my teenage years, and naturally, I would have liked to dress well, as many other friends in the class and hostel did. I had a limited amount of money, as no one at home had any fixed income. During term time, most of the time I had only 5 rupees to spend, and that included bus fare to go home (75 cents from Kekirawa to Yakalla) at the end of the term. These were the years when artificial fabrics like nylon and terylene shirts appeared for sale. Some students in the hostel had them and talked about how quickly those shirts dry after washing, and there was no need for ironing. A washerman would come to the hostel and take away students' clothes for washing and ironing or ironing only. It cost a small fee for these services. As I did not have any extra money to spare, I used to fold my shirt and keep it under my pillow, so that next morning it looked somewhat like an ironed shirt. During the rainy season, I had another problem. It was very difficult to dry clothes and sometimes I wore slightly wet clothes to school. Eventually the clothes dried because of body temperature. Once when Sudu *Akka* came home, she bought me a nylon shirt which was a treasured gift.

Life went on without any great changes, centred around school and hostel or home and working either in the home garden or paddy field at either Huruluwewa or Yakalla during school holidays. It finally came to the year that I sat for the GCE (OL) public examination. For the first time, I had my photograph taken at Kekirawa studio for the identity card that we had to carry to the examination hall. I passed the GCE (OL) with six credits, and we were placed in the GCE (AL) class, but there were no qualified teachers in the school.

After the results came I went home, as many others did. Typically, we walked from Yakalla to Padikaramaduwa, which was about seven kilometres, as there was no regular bus service. Punchi *Akka* had seen me walking home and come hurriedly from the weaving centre. She asked whether I had passed the examination. I told her I had passed with six credits, and with a big sigh of relief, she shed a tear. She likely thought all their hard work had been worth it. Six credits was not common in those days, particularly in the science stream.

Punchi *Akka* came home with me. I talked about those who passed the GCE leaving the school, as there were no teachers. Most of them went to Matale, Kandy and some to Kurunegala. Those who went to better schools had at least some relatives or family connection there, so most of them stayed with a relative. My friends Kamalaratne and Jinna went to Matale Science College and Kamalaratne stayed in a relative's house. Jinna and another friend, Sumanaratne, stayed in a private boarding house as they had the means to pay. Matale Science College was a reputable school, but there was no hostel at the time and I couldn't afford to pay a private boarding school. We discussed all these aspects at home. My brother told me not to study further and to find a job so that everyone at home would be relieved. But I was determined to study further and explained there was no point in stopping now. The following day I went to the school and met up with Nimal. He had failed the exam. Headmaster Mr Sirisena and the headmistress were very happy that I had passed, since they treated me like their own child. Nimal and I decided to study together in every school holiday as it would help him, and we did.

People usually talking about one turning point in their lives, but I had many. I talked to Yakalla *Akka* about the school in Matale, and also Nugawela (Central College). She said it was a good area to live and gave me 5 rupees to go to Matale and find the school. That was her quality – she would give anything without hesitation if it brought any good to her siblings or children. This was the first turning point; without that 5 rupees, I might not have found a school. The following morning, I took the Kahatagasdigiliya-Kandy bus which came to Yakalla around 7.30 am, so I had to come very early in the morning from Padikaramaduwa. I had never been to Matale before. After getting off the bus in Matale, I asked various people to help me find the school.

I went straight to the principal's office, showed him the letter containing my GCE (OL) results and asked about the possibility of getting admission to the GCE (AL) mathematics class. The principal was Mr A Bopitiya, who had written a geometry textbook, and he was a very kind person. He called in the head of mathematics, Mr Kapilaratne, who refused to take any more students, stating that the class was super-full at the time. Naturally, Science College attracted many students from all over the country. However, on the principal's guarantee that this was the last admission, and due to the fact I had good results and had come a long way seeking admission, Mr Kapilaratne agreed to take me into the class. This was the second turning point.

After further discussion with Mr Bopitiya about transferring my scholarship, he prepared a letter and asked me to go to the offices of the Department of Education. I walked through the town, asking people where the Education Department was and finally found it. There, I showed the letter given to me by the principal and met the head of the department and talked about transferring the scholarship. He suggested there was nothing they could do, as it was the responsibility of the Director of Education in Anuradhapura. He prepared a letter stating they were willing to accept the scholarship and administer it from the Matale office. I was hungry that day, but never spent a single cent. I came home and the following morning went to the Kekirawa hostel.

After arriving at the hostel, some school friends asked whether I had found a school. I told the story and one of my friends, Wegodapola, told me the easiest way would be to meet the Kekirawa Member of Parliament (MP) Mr Lenawa and tell him. He would ask the Director of Education to transfer the scholarship. The following morning, I went to Mr Lenawa's house along the Kekirawa–Yakalla road. When I entered, he was sitting at the dining table for breakfast, dressed in white national clothes. His maid brought out a large *roti* bread, which is one of my favourite foods. As I greedily watched him eat, Mr Lenawa asked, 'Why is this boy here?' I explained the need for my scholarship transfer to Matale. His reply was that I shouldn't go anywhere. He said, 'I'm going to talk to your principal. We will start advanced level science stream classes soon and I will get some teachers.' He told me he was about to catch the train to Colombo to attend parliamentary sessions and on his return he would talk with the principal, and then added, 'If good students leave, we may never be able to develop the school.'

On hearing this, my world collapsed, and I went back to the school hostel and decided to go to Anuradhapura to meet the Director of Education. With all the necessary documents in hand, I took the early morning bus to Anuradhapura and went to the *kachcheri* (now the district secretary's office) where the Education Department was located. Not knowing the formalities in meeting senior government officials, I tried to enter the Director's office straight away, but the peon who was sitting in front stopped me and chased me out. He said I had to make an appointment, and it was not easy for everyone to meet the Director. I begged him, but there was no sympathy and he chased me out once again.

Behind me, I heard a familiar voice saying, 'Senevi, what you are doing here?' To my surprise, it was the school's Buddhist priest who had taken our Buddhism classes in year 8. I explained everything to him and he took me to the Director and got the scholarship transfer letter organised immediately. This was the third turning point.

There was no adult in my family capable of helping me to find a school, no relatives or any known person, but with determination and a bit of luck, all worked out well. The 5 rupees given me by Yakalla *Akka*, the kindness of Mr Bopitiya, and the intervention of the school priest at the right moment were the three main turning points in my life.

There was one big problem I needed to sort out before I could start at the Science College. The money … to buy textbooks, to buy white long trousers, shirts and at least one pair of black shoes. The cost was at least a hundred rupees. In addition, as the hostel was not yet open, I needed to find a place to stay. Adasooriya *Aiya*'s niece lived in her husband's house about two kilometres from Matale town centre in Elwala, and Yakalla *Akka* had talked to them; they agreed I could stay at their house. There was no one with a hundred rupees in my family and *Amma* suggested writing to Sudu *Akka*. It might be six months' salary, and even if she did send it, it would take time to arrange and could be too late to attend the school in time. Abandoning that idea, *Amma* suggested leasing one acre from the rice field for next season to get the money, and she managed to lease to Sivurala who lived in *Aba* colony. The lease agreement was very dear, as we had to allow him one season to cultivate and then subsequent seasons until we paid him the leased amount of 100 rupees back.

After several months at Elwala, I moved into the school hostel. Life at the hostel was conducive to studying. I had a number of good friends in my class and they were all keen to enter the university. The only problem was that some daily scholars were aligned with the underground movement of the Janatha Vimukthi Peramuna (JVP) who conducted classes on how to liberate the country from imperial ruling parties. We were asked to join, sometimes with threats. Finally, I joined the movement and went to five classes, but was not actively involved beyond that. On 5th April 1971, JVP attacked police stations island wide and apparently their liberation struggle had started. The school and hostel were closed, and we were asked to return to our homes. I didn't have enough money, so the school gave us all five rupees each for our bus fare. Packing clothes and books, we left the hostel, but the bus service was poor. Police checks were everywhere along the road.

It was late evening by the time we arrived at Kekirawa town and found there was no bus service to Yakalla along Kekirawa–Kahatagasdigiliya road until the following day. There were a couple of others looking for overnight accommodation as well, and we found a shop owner who kindly allowed us to stay in his shed about two kilometres out of town. We assured him we were students and had no link to JVP.

The following day, I went first to Yakalla. When I got there, I found Yakalla *Akka* crying since I had not arrived home the previous day. Everyone was overjoyed to see me back home in Huruluwewa. It was a long holiday. Because of the closure of schools island-wide, Nimal and Wimal were staying with their parents. It was a good time to catch up with them. We did some studying, but talked more about the situation in the country. There were many rumours as some parts of the country were under JVP rule and a lot of assassinations were reported. Yakalla *Akka* came to stay with us with her children for safety and only Adasooriya *Aiya* went to Yakalla daily to look after and protect the house. During this time, a friend gave me a print- out of Rudyard Kiplings' *IF–* and it has been my guiding light ever since.

After three months, schjool restarted. A year later in April 1972, I sat for the GCE (AL) examination and went home. We all applied for the newly created teaching positions that had opened for teaching science at schools. In the meantime, I started growing vegetables with Siriya, who lived next door. We prepared the rice field as there had been no rice cultivation the previous year. We dug a well, fenced off the area, built a hut, walked around fields collecting cow manure, and prepared the land. Siriya suggested we grow marketable upcountry vegetables, such as cabbage, carrot, tomato, turnip, beetroot and leek. With cow manure as fertiliser and twice a day watering, after a month, we had established a lush vegetable garden among the barren-dry paddy fields. It was the talking point of the village. As we had to protect the vegetables from thieves and wandering cattle, we stayed overnight in the hut there. When it was necessary, only one would go home at any one time while the other looked after the plot.

Amidst all this happening, the long-awaited letter arrived stating that I had been appointed as the science teacher at the Huruluwewa Wamivura Mahavidyalaya. The salary was 220 rupees per month, which was good. The school was along the Yakalla–Galenbiduniwewa road, about three kilometres from Yakalla. To reach the school, I had to come another seven kilometres from Padikaramaduwa and I had to be at school by 7.30 am which meant leaving the house very early in the morning. There was no school uniform, so at least there was no issue around buying clothes. The bus from Padikaramaduwa was not regular and some days I walked to Yakalla and from there took the bus to the school. I thought of buying a bicycle, but there were no savings among us. Mother heard there was an old bicycle available for sale for 60 rupees at Ukkubanda *Wedamahaththaya*'s house and went there to borrow it until I got my salary, but he refused. Mother asked him daily, but the jealous *Wedamaththaya* did not want to give it up. Several months passed, and I either took the erratic bus from Padikaramaduwa to Yakalla or walked until I could finally buy a new bicycle. The salary I earned I brought home and gave to Punchi *Akka* to take care of, and she managed it very well. With Kumari *Nangi*, I prepared a list of things that we going to do with the savings: how much to spend on groceries, how much to spend on clothes and other necessities, how much to lease other people's rice fields for us to cultivate, and even how much to expand the house.

Life at the school as a teacher was interesting. There was another trained science teacher and a mathematics teacher there, too. I taught general science for years 7 and 8 and physics for GCE (OL) classes (years 9 and 10). Some of the children did not have books or pencils in the lower classes, so I would regularly spend 10 to 20 rupees on these necessities for children's education. The school principal, Mr Ananda Herath, was also from Huruluwewa and lived in the school bungalow. He and his wife, Lily Herath, were very kind to me and treated me as their own brother. Mr Herath also had attended Padikaramaduwa school as I had. There were lots of one-day training courses for new teachers introducing the new mathematics and science curricula. From these courses, I met most of my school friends and we all enjoyed renewed friendships.

The economy at home was somewhat improved with a stable income, and everyone was happy. On my first attempt, I could not enter the university and this came as a blessing in disguise, as I could continue working as a teacher and save some more money. On my second attempt in 1973, I qualified to enter the following year in the Faculty of Engineering at the University of Sri Lanka, Katubedda Campus, and in 1978, I graduated as a civil engineer.

Being born poor is not something to be ashamed of,
but striving to achieve success and helping
others is something to be proud of.

-Nara Somaratne-

Chapter 3

Fulfillment of family responsibilities

Life at university wasn't easy. Initially, I shared accommodation with some friends, but money was scarce. Breakfast might be a sugar bun or sometimes nothing, lunch was at the university canteen and dinner was anything available at a nearby shop. A number of my batchmates were old school friends: Justin, Piya, Jaya and Nimal were among them. In addition, Rane and Sarath became close friends. By this time Sudu *Akka* was working in a house in Kotte area as a domestic servant, and later she joined a private hospital as a cook. I used to visit her whenever I got a break. For my sustenance, I applied for the higher education bank loan, which was enough if carefully managed. Knowing Punchi *Akka*'s economic theory – 'if only one who earns a rupee knows how to spend a rupee' – I carefully managed the stipend received from the loan, so life went on as usual. Hardships were not new to me. My only aim was to graduate and get employment. I was never involved in political or love affairs during the university period.

After the final year examination, I went to see the Dean of the Faculty to obtain a letter as I had completed all required examinations and was awaiting results. This letter was required as evidence of qualifications to a prospective employer. There was some talk among friends about possible organisations that might have vacancies. One such organisation was the Mahaweli Development Board. I took the bus to Bambalapitiya junction and walked up to Jawatte Road, where the head office was located. Eventually I met the general manager, Mr Rajanathan, who asked me from where I come from. I told him I was from Huruluwewa. He started to act more friendly after that and told me he was involved in construction works on the Huruluwewa scheme as a young engineer and he was supervising the building of a causeway across the Yan Oya which I knew of. Mr Rajanathan told me he would post me to a place close to Huruluwewa and asked his secretary to prepare the documents immediately.

So, my first employment was as a civil engineer on Mahaweli river development work at Kalawewa project and we were attached to the Eppawala resident engineer's office. I went there soon after the November 1978 cyclone. All along the road from Huruluwewa to Eppawala, there were fallen trees and destruction to buildings and power lines. I reported for duty late afternoon and the chief resident engineer was very kind and explained the type of works that we would carry out and about our accommodation.

We lived in shared accommodation provided at the camp. There were several engineers with us, some from Peradeniya University. I was the only one from Katubedda. I met Gune, who used to study at the school in Matale. There were several others: Raja, Ganesh, Mervin, Loku, Siva and several technical staff in other dormitories. Among the technical staff, Sena was my closest friend. The work was divided between office and field works involving the design and construction of irrigation canals, road networks and small dams. At the time, we were paid a healthy salary, subsistence and overtime for long working hours, almost six to seven days a week. After dinner, we would chat about anything and everything, play some cards and occasionally sing and record. I was a pathetic singer and even now,

I cannot listen to the records. Some weekends, we would go for little tours around the district sightseeing, visiting historical places and ruins, and watch wild elephants in forested areas. I bought a camera and photography became my hobby.

The area we worked was a typical rural setting, open lands and pockets of villages in between. The open lands were once forest areas people had used as *chena* cultivation and then abandoned. New irrigation canals ran through lowlands in these areas and highlands were reserved for human settlement and divided into allotments. Every one of the engineers worked tirelessly to achieve targets, and I was one of the high achievers.

Alongside the hard work, our enjoyment of life was second to none. At least once a month we had a get-together, usually on a Saturday night at either Illuppallama or at Kalawewa circuit bungalows. Sometimes the organisers would invite the engineers from nearby areas and the gathering would be up to fifty people. Drinks and food were served for a nominal fee, and the talking and singing would go on until dawn. We were able to relax, and everyone enjoyed themselves at these evening gatherings. This was one of the very happy periods in my life.

Meantime, living conditions on the home front improved dramatically, as I was earning a good salary. After I received my first pay, I went home with lots of presents bought from Kekirawa: clothes for *Amma*, my sisters, brother, nephews and nieces. I bought sweets for the little ones. It was difficult to carry it all on the bus, so I bought a large bag and packed it all into it. As I got down from the bus, I went straight to my elder sister's house in Yakalla. No words can describe her emotion, seeing the tears in her eyes, her pride in my achievements. I took the evening bus to go to Huruluwewa and everyone was happy to see me, and I talked about the work we were doing and life at Eppawala.

By this time, my youngest sister Kumari was studying at the Peradeniya University, and she came home in April for Sinhala new year holiday. We discussed how to improve the family economy by leasing rice fields and cultivating them and making various small investments. The most important part of our planning was arranging the marriages of Punchi *Akka*, who was over 32 years of age, and finding a bride for my brother, who was just two years older than me. We talked about arranging a wedding for younger sister Seela as well. By this time, she had fallen in love with Kumara at her workplace. Kumara was a gentleman with sober habits and worked as a chief cake decorator in one of the prominent cake factories in Colombo. One of Kumara's natural talents was fine art – be it decorating cakes, drawing, or any kind of crafts – he excelled at it. There were many responsibilities I had to fulfill, and improving and expanding the house and educating Yakalla *Akka*'s children were a priority. As I had to come home often, I bought a motorcycle so I could balance my time between home and workplace. Kumara and Seela's wedding took place in 1979. This was one of my first big responsibilities.

Gune and several other friends at work told me not to accumulate salary in a bank account as the interest was very low. They advised investing with them on several projects and this proved to give a good return. As it was my childhood dream to take the family back to the ancestral village in Kurunegala, I saved very carefully to purchase land and build a house. Meantime I started to buy jewelries for my sisters. Typically, this is a father's responsibility in Sri Lankan society, but since we didn't have a father, I fulfilled it. I bought my mother a gold necklace and two bangles. On that day her eyes were filled with tears of joy; this was the first time she had worn gold jewelry.

Meantime at the workplace in Eppawala, we were also busy with wedding arrangements. Almost all my friends had girlfriends from their university days and Gune fell in love with a girl in the area. He frequently visited there to arrange his wedding. Most of my other friends visited their homes or their fiancées homes on weekends. Our chief engineer, Sarath, was a well-mannered gentleman. He was more than a leader, and at times when one needed help, he offered it like one's own brother. Everyone appreciated this quality in him. He was a health-conscious person, and he organised exercise programs and swimming in village tanks and the main canal, and he never missed social gatherings, whether they were near or faraway camps. Life was very relaxed, and everyone enjoyed it.

By 1980, I had sufficient funds to purchase land and build a house, and I frequently visited Kurunegala to find suitable land. However, I couldn't find suitable land or a house in our ancestral village in Kannehepola, so I bought a house in Mallawapitiya off Kurunegala-Kandy Road. It became the family house for the next two decades. Meanwhile, a suitable bride for my brother was proposed from neighbouring Nikawewa. The family originally came from Kandy district. After my brother's wedding, my mother and elder sister Punchi *Akka* came to settle down in the Mallawapitiya house with niece Arty who grew up in our house from early childhood. I would go there on weekends and look after my family. Amid all these happening I also went to work in the Colombo head office to gain engineering design experience, which was a prerequisite to gaining professional qualifications.

Following my design experience, I started working at Maduru Oya development project in Polonnaruwa district. I stayed in Aralaganwila camp sharing a house with Karu, Nissanka, Sam and Wella. Life was, as before, very enjoyable. Gune married his girlfriend and had a daughter and was living in a separate house. We had a nice housekeeper called Aththe, who was paid as a casual labourer. He prepared our meals, cleaned the house, did the shopping and sometimes washed my clothes, for which I paid him extra money as a gift. At least once a fortnight, on weekends, I went home to see my mother. The work was similar to what I had done on the Kala Oya development project, so I didn't gain any new experience. The chief engineer's name was Shelton. During that time, the Maduru Oya dam and associated main canals were under construction by overseas contracting companies, and the company staff lived in a separate camp close to the dam.

Whenever we had a break or on the weekend, we would go to Pasikuda beach or to visit our friends on the Ulhitiya project. Nissanka usually organised our trips, and we also went to Pigeon Island, Trincomalee, Kumana National Park to watch the birds and wildlife, Batticaloa, hill country to see waterfalls, Hambantota and Kataragama. Our friend Wella, who lived with us, would usually go home to see his wife and kids who lived in Colombo. We almost covered the eastern province of the country and I enjoyed capturing very much the scenery and wildlife as I was very keen on photography. I developed the habit of carrying my camera bag wherever I went. The life was most enjoyable balancing work–family responsibilities and watching wildlife and taking photos. Photography was my hobby.

Family Is for Life

In life, there are few constants.
We face the ebb and flow.
Situations happen.
People come and go.
But when you count your blessings
You'll see, in joy and strife,
One thing you can rely on;
Family is for life!

-Ms Moem-

Chapter 4

Marriage and troubles begin

By 1981, my remaining friends and colleagues, who were in their mid- to late-twenties, were either married or busy with wedding arrangements. It was like waves in the ocean: when one wedding passed, another wedding arrived. Sometimes friends joked that 'Senevi is wave resistant,' for not even having had a girlfriend yet. I just laughed, knowing my responsibilities towards the family. Once again, there were a few marriage proposals that came through friends – some were from their own villages, or from families they knew, even from their wives' friends. I simply delayed, not giving straight answers as I had an elder sister and younger sister yet to marry. I needed to fulfill this responsibility before thinking about myself. Finally, the 'wave of marriage' reached our quarters. Karu's brother-in-law had arranged a bride for him. She was a schoolteacher from Tennekumbura close to Kandy. Karu said both families visited each other and agreed upon the marriage. He frequently visited home to see his future wife. Nissanka was getting ready to marry his childhood girlfriend from his hometown down south. Upali took a transfer to the Colombo office to arrange his wedding as his girlfriend worked there.

I could not attend Karu's wedding as I had to go to my batchmate's wedding in Negombo. After the wedding, Karu and his bride, Deepa, came and stayed with us until their house was ready to occupy. Deepa was quite nice and a kind person. We had to be on our best behaviour and act well-mannered as a lady was living in the house. Often, at home we went shirtless, but now we had to cover up; at meals times, we had to wait until everyone was ready and talk in a low voice. After Karu and Deepa left for their new accommodation in Manampitiya, a new engineer, Keerthi, came in and occupied Karu's room. Keerthi was a quiet person and an environmental enthusiast, and he quite eagerly joined me to go and watch birds, see the floods during the rainy season, and watch wild elephants in the nearby national park. It felt as though he was a younger brother. Karu and Deepa visited us one day and asked us to visit them whenever we could as there were no neighbours for them to talk to. Whenever we had time after work or even when we visited Polonnaruwa, we would never forget to stopover at Karu's place. Sometimes we stayed for dinner and Deepa very happily prepared delicious meals for us. One day I said, 'It is nice to have a meal prepared from a "hand with bangles".'

'You can one day have a "hand with bangles" to prepare your meal,' said both Karu and Deepa together.

'Hahaha, yes, one day,' was my answer.

'Seriously, there is a girl from Kandy who is Deepa's classmate,' Karu said. 'There is a proposal to her from Wariyapola, one of your senior batches.'

I asked what she did, and Deepa gave a long answer. 'Her name is Suramya and she is currently attending chemistry external classes as she could not enter the university. The classes are run by the university, and she can get an external degree. She is a good housekeeper.'

'Why is she going to classes and at the same time looking for a marriage?' I asked.

'Probably to grab whichever comes first,' Karu laughed. Then he seriously asked, 'What sort of a girl are you looking for?'

'Not from a rich family, but from a good family,' I said. 'It would be good to have one with a teaching type job but not an office environment. Not having a job is also OK so long as she's a good girl and can look after my family.'

'My friend is coming from a good family,' said Deepa. 'We were in the same class. Several times I visited her home. Her father died when she was a little girl, maybe ten years old, and thereafter her elder brother Dayananda looked after her like a father. Dayananda works in Colombo as a senior staff member in an embassy and his wife and two little kids live in their house in Udahagama which is close to Peradeniya. Suramya is also helping to raise the brother's children, and one day, it will be easy for you as she already has this experience. She is even good at looking after paddy fields …'

'Can she plough a paddy field?' I said. 'We have a paddy field in Huruluwewa.'

We all laughed at that. 'No, no …' Deepa intervened. 'I meant preparation of tea and lunch for workers in the field. Is that what you mean by … ? I think she can work with a mamoty and cleaning bunds, though and pull the plough and transplant rice crops.'

Deepa was a little embarrassed, and we stopped teasing her.

'What do you think?' Nissanka asked.

'I really do not want to marry from a family with lots of younger siblings as it will be an additional burden to me looking after two families.' I went on to tell them about my family background and responsibilities and that I did not want to run into any trouble.

This time, Deepa gave a little more detail. 'She is very serious, Suramya – the youngest child and the only girl in the family. She has three elder brothers. Dayananda works in Colombo and she calls him Daya *Aiya*. He is married to Chitra, and Suramya calls her Chitra *Akka*. She is also from the Kandy area.' Deepa said they were both very pleasant and nice people. She said Chitra *Akka* was a typical Kandiyan woman, and wore a Kandiyan saree around the home.

I mentioned I would one day like for my wife to wear a Kandiyan saree at home, being a traditional village man myself.

'She would, if you asked, as it is not a new habit for them,' Deepa said, continuing to give more details. 'Suramya's second elder brother, Nandimitra, is married, and her name is Nelum, and they live close by. The third one lives in Australia. I know nothing about them, but Dayananda and Chitra are quite nice people.'

'Well,' Nissanka said, 'why don't you make a visit? What do you think? At least you will have a nice lunch.'

'I have already had several nice lunches,' I said, 'but I do not mind another one.'

Deepa said she would write to her and arrange a date.

So, it went on. In March 1983, Gune, Karu, Deepa and I went to Kandy to visit Suramya's place. First of all, we went to Deepa's home at Tennekumbura and had a late lunch. Then in the evening we went to Suramya's home. Suramya's mother, elder brother Dayananda and his wife Chitra were there waiting for us. Dayananda asked us about life in Polonnaruwa and how we spent our weekends. He asked whether I went home every weekend. Meanwhile, Deepa went into the dining area and came out with Suramya and presented her to us. She was shy, and we did not talk, but Karu introduced all of us as he had visited before. Then her elder brother left us and she was alone with us. I asked Suramya about her chemistry classes, and she said it was an external course but recognised by the university so she could sit for an external degree.

Several months passed quietly until I accidentally met Suramya at Deepa's house. Following this, I took my mother and younger sister to Suramya's place. Suramya's mother asked about family details and what was the father's job. To which my sister Kumari gave a straight answer, telling her that father had been a poor farmer and we lived in Huruluwewa as father had sold our lands in our Kurunegala ancestral village.

Two weeks later, Suramya's family, Dayananda and Chitra, Nandimitra and Nelum and Suramya's mother visited our place at Mallawapitiya. I asked Nissanka to come and stay with us on the day to keep the conversation going. They had lunch, and before leaving the house, Nandimitra told me I could visit Suramya so we could get to know each other. This was typically the way of acknowledging they would like to go ahead with the marriage proposal.

Meantime, one of our family friends brought a proposal to my elder sister Punchi *Akka*. He was from a village close to Alawwa and a gentleman of sober habits who worked in a desiccated coconut processing factory. Then my younger sister Kumari started working in a government corporation in Colombo.

Every weekend, I would visit Suramya and discuss various things. I told her we had to be honest with each other. I told her I had had a short-lived love affair with a close relative and had to stop within two weeks as everyone opposed it. Suramya also said she had a love affair a long time ago with Chitra *Akka*'s younger brother, Wickrama, and also stopped as her mother opposed it. I asked her what she was going to do with her chemistry classes if she was going to marry. She said she has already decided to stop as it was very difficult to continue after marriage as she was not sure where she was going to live. I said initially it would be in Maduru Oya as I had already applied for a separate house from the camp. I asked her one day if I did not have a job, how were we going to live and asked what she would do. She said, 'We will think about that at the time, not now,' and laughed. I explained to her my journey through life, about my time in Huruluwewa and our ancestral village, and in detail, about my family and responsibilities. She said Daya *Aiya* had already told her after I had spoken to him. Daya *Aiya* said to her that Senevi was like their father – he had achieved success from nothing – but Senevi was more than that as their father did not have any siblings.

Suramya started to wear the Kandyan saree whenever I came to see her, and she said she liked to wear it like Chitra *Akka*. By this time, Suramya had become a close friend. One day Nandimitra and I were in the front yard, and as he pointed to some distant rice fields, he said, 'That is the rice field we are giving to Suramya and there is another plot of land as well.'

I told him I have six sisters and we never even thought about a dowry, and that I could manage our lives without one. Later, Suramya told me he had told this to others in the family, and they were all very happy about my decision. On weekends when I was there, Nandimitra and Nelum, with their children Sugandhika and Keerthi, visited and we got to know each other. Talking about our accidental meeting at Deepa's house, Suramya said soon after she came home, Nelum *Akka* had said to her, 'Tell me everything that happened!' Suramya asked her what about. After coming home, Sugandhika had said, 'Today we met the uncle who is going to marry Suramya aunty.' Obviously, on the way back home, Sugandhika might have asked 'who was that we met?' and Suramya might have answered 'that is the uncle that I am going to marry.' Otherwise, a little girl would not be able to guess. Both Sugandhika and her younger brother Keerthi were pleasant kids and good readers. Daya *Aiya* and Chitra *Akka* also had two little children, Nandana and Nandani, both younger than Keerthi. By this time, I had met most of Suramya's relatives, as they visited often upon hearing the news that Suramya was getting ready for marriage.

One day, Nandimitra told me they had decided to have the marriage registration in October and the wedding in November. I was surprised to hear that and wondered why it was happening in a hurry, but I was not told anything as to why. It was a busy time. Nandimitra took charge of everything at Suramya's house and my younger sister Kumari did the same from our house. By this time, the wedding arrangements were taking place for my elder sister, Punchi *Akka*. Even though her marriage had been delayed, everyone was happy she had finally found a good person. He was also visiting our home every weekend, but I could not be there as I was visiting at Suramya's place.

After our engagement, and before the wedding of Punchi *Akka* and Nilame *Aiya's* marriage registration was undertaken at our home. I provided every detail to Suramya, as she was very interested to hear about it. I was very happy about it. Meantime Suramya started to tell me more about her family. She said again and again that of the three brothers, she was closest to Daya *Aiya*. The youngest of her elder brothers, Kumara, was living in Australia and married to an Italian lady called Mina. They had met in Italy while Kumara was studying at an Italian university. After studying in Italy and marriage, Kumara and Mina immigrated to Australia, and Suramya had not seen them for years. I told her I felt closest to Nandimitra as he was the one I frequently met. I liked Daya *Aiya* too, but he was just like me – a bit reserved and didn't talk much. Suramya laughed and said Daya *Aiya* and Chitra *Akka* were the best and asked me to deal with Nandimitra carefully, particularly when it came to money matters. She said Daya *Aiya* used to come home weekends to spend time with his wife and children, but Nandimitra always accompanied him to Kandy and came home in the evening after having lots of drinks. He took advantage of Daya *Aiya*'s kindness. Nelum *Akka* was also like that, she said. Whenever a family event occurred, whether it was a new year celebration or any alms giving, she would only attend at the last minute. She avoided everything and gave nothing. Nandimitra would give them an excuse that Nelum couldn't come as she was suffering from wheezing. It was a popular excuse that everyone was familiar with. They could even forecast when she would get the wheezing again. Unlike Nelum, Chitra *Akka* joined the family for anything and everything, as she was a down-to-earth woman.

Both Nandimitra and Nelum had opposed the marriage of Daya *Aiya* and Chitra *Akka* and they have even told her mother not to go ahead with it. As Daya *Aiya* was educated and did his post-graduate studies in Japan, and was doing a good job, maybe they thought that Chitra *Akka* was not good enough, but she was the perfect woman for him. Ever since, Nelum had cursed Chitra *Akka*. Nelum's mother was also like that – arrogant, living with hatred and very unpopular in the village. She also kept one of the husband's younger brothers as a second husband. The children belonged to both of them. That was practising polyandry, which had been abolished during the British rule. Suramya said sarcastically, 'The funny thing is, Nelum was our first cousin; matter of fact, she is my mother's elder sister's daughter.'

Suramya also talked about her close relatives in the village, some of whom I had already met. There were several family friends, among them Weerasekara who frequently visited, as he was a close friend of Nandimitra. He was popularly known as Weera *Aiya*. He would usually stay overnight at Nandimitra's house but, some time ago, he had boarded at Suramya's place. He was also a graduate teacher and one of those friends who got together for drinks at a Colombo Street bar in Kandy with Nandimitra and Dayananda.

Chitra *Akka* was the eldest in that family. She had two younger brothers, Perakum and Wickrama and youngest sister was Renu. Suramya explained that Chitra *Akka*'s family were their relatives, and she had frequently stayed with them to attend her degree course. She still called him Daya *Aiya* as before. Her mother had proposed Chitra *Akka* to Daya *Aiya* and after that, up until their marriage, she never came to stay. Renu *Akka* was two years older than Suramya, and more than relatives, they were close friends. She was also a graduate and worked somewhere in Polonnaruwa. After our engagement, Daya *Aiya* took his family to Colombo. Perakum found a place to rent with one of his friends, a businessman's house, to share. Daya *Aiya*'s family lived upstairs, and they visited Kandy on weekends.

When I visited Suramya, we would sit on the veranda outside the house. After our engagement, one day Suramya said that after the wedding she couldn't stay in either her house or in our house. I told her the house at the camp I had applied for was almost ready and would be furnished soon. Suramya said she frequently fought and quarreled with her mother. Sometimes her mother passed hints to Chitra *Akka*, even though her mother was the one who proposed to Daya *Aiya*. Every week, by Friday evening, everyone showed a happy face as if nothing had happened because Daya *Aiya* was coming home for the weekend.

Suramya looked sad and said there was nothing wrong with Chitra *Akka* but her mother always found something to hurt her. At new year's when everyone gave presents to her mother, she hurt Suramya by saying, 'I may not get any present from you as you cannot get a job.' It was terrible when she put her down in front of others, whether siblings or relatives. On another occasion, she said to Suramya, 'You may never get married because of your rough skin.' Suramya rubbed the tears from her eyes. I was surprised how a mother could say this to her own daughter. Suramya cried and I felt miserable and helpless and said, 'Now you can buy presents for her; you *are* going to have a husband, and don't worry about your skin!'

Suramya said that she did not have many clothes or much jewellery either. She had only two necklaces and a couple of sarees to wear. She would never ask her brothers – and nor had they offered any help, but her brother in Australia was sending money to buy whatever she wanted for the wedding. For other expenses, they had sold the family rice field. On the way home that evening, I thought what a miserable mother she had, and that Suramya had suffered because of her mother's arrogant behaviour. She said her father was a very kind person, but she had lost him when she was just ten years old. He worked away at distance places and came to Kandy only very close to his retirement. I was becoming closer and closer to her and offered every kind word to please her, giving hope for our future. It was now my responsibility looking after her welfare. I was determined to make her life comfortable.

Time passed quickly, and soon the wedding took place on 17th November 1983. I took Suramya to Nuwara Eliya for honeymoon and she thoroughly enjoyed the time we had. My younger sister, Kumari, was the one who organised everything for the homecoming. After the homecoming, we stayed a few days at our home and went back to her home in Udahagama in Kandy. After visiting a few close relatives, we came back to Kurunegala to visit my close relatives. There were many places to visit, but we postponed the wedding visits and went back to Maduru Oya to start my work. Suramya enjoyed the time in Maduru Oya. Whenever I had time, I showed her around – peacocks in the campsite, wild elephants in the adjacent national park, and Maduru Oya dam and canals where we worked.

When Suramya's mother visited us with Nandimitra and family, I took them on an enjoyable outing to the Ulhitiya project area and to visit the Dambana *Veddah* people (aboriginals in Sri Lanka). On our way back, a wild elephant was on the road coming straight towards our vehicle. The driver was well-experienced in this type of situation and stopped the vehicle and waited until the elephant moved away. The elephant came so close to the vehicle, almost striking distance, and stayed there for nearly 30 minutes before moving into the shrubs. This experience was a first for all of them, particularly little Sugandhika and Keerthi, who kept talking about how their grandmother was shivering and praying.

At least every second weekend, we came home to complete our wedding visits and to arrange Punchi *Akka*'s wedding. One day, when we returned from a visit, I was driving towards Peradeniya from Kandy and talking about the number of places we still had to visit. Almost suddenly, Suramya changed the subject and started to talk about Weera *Aiya* for no obvious reason.

'Weera *Aiya* once married and she was a schoolteacher,' she said. 'They both had strong personalities and because of this, finally after a few months, they had to divorce. That is what happens when both are strong and only one in the family needs to be strong.'

I was surprised why my young bride wanted to say this within a month of our marriage. It appeared that she was indirectly telling me to listen to her; she must have control of our affairs. At the time, I simply ignored this comment but later realised she really meant it. On the twentieth day after our marriage, we were in Suramya's house. I was in the room and Suramya walked angrily in and out of the room and in again. I asked what had happened? She was angry and started to scold me, saying 'what a husband I have …' and so on. I once again asked why and what had happened, as there was no apparent reason for this behaviour.

'This is not the way newly married couples live,' I said. 'We must be happy. Look at the other married people and how they live; this is the best time of our lives.'

To this she replied straight-cut: 'How do we know how other people live? They may also live like this – we do not know for sure.' She was quarrelling with me. This was completely unexpected; I had not been engaged in quarrelling with anyone before. I said, 'Please keep quiet, and please do not let me lose my love and respect for you.'

As she continued yelling, I once again asked her to at least tell me why.

'You smoke,' she said.

'You knew that from my day one, didn't you?' We had discussed it before, so why were we now quarrelling about it? 'Your two brothers smoke and all three drink alcohol,' I continued, 'this is not something new to you …'

'Mother always says, "Fix your husband the way you want."'

This was her answer. I couldn't believe it. Why would Suramya want to quarrel with me about smoking when she could talk in a more friendly way? Why would her mother advise her daughter to fix her husband to do things the way she wants? Why would Suramya's mother not tell her three daughters-in-law to fix their husbands, her own sons? Why me? I could smell something sinister was going on. Out of her three sons, two were smokers and all of them drank alcohol, so why could she not stop this? Despite all these questions arising, I knew not to agitate Suramya. After all, it was within one month of the marriage. However, I was determined not to be subservient to my wife as her mother expected me to be. That would be ridiculous. However, I tolerated the situation without getting into an argument.

When Suramya became angry, she always kept a frown on her face and replied back using sharp words such as 'How do I know…?', 'I do not know …' or even simple words such as 'yes' and 'no' in different tones. She had a peculiar walk when she became angry too, walking fast and making a peculiar *thud-thud* sound as she stepped.

One morning, she started to walk angrily and was not talking to me. I asked her, 'Is there anything wrong?' She didn't reply straight away and moved away from me, saying, 'What a man I have married.' That weekend, Dayananda's family came home. Little later Suramya's school friend Priyani, a medical practitioner in the Kandy area, came and was talking with everyone in the family. She had been a frequent visitor. I went to check where Suramya was and heard she was talking to Priyani in a small room of the house. As I was just about to enter the room, I heard Suramya telling Priyani, 'This man has nothing else to do except help his Kurunegala dirty family (Kurunegala *Heththata Kaburanawa misak*). It is apparent she was criticising me to her friend. My world collapsed, and it became very clear to me what her mother had asked her to fix – to remove me from my family.

All this happening within two months of marriage. I was helpless and sought the help of Dayananda.

After lunch I told Dayananda what I had heard, and he called Suramya and scolded her saying, 'We all knew *Malli* had to look after his family and we all three brothers talked about it and appreciate what he is doing. What is wrong with you? Tell me now? Why did you tell that to Priyani, and who is she anyway? If you genuinely had any problems, you should have talked to us – at least you could tell Chitra. We smoke, we drink, we help our family, and why can't you see that? Why do you want to control your husband?'

Suramya was quiet at the time, but she continued her own way, anyway. It caused me a great deal of pain when she called my family *Heththa* (filthy people). After all, it was my mother and siblings who helped me achieve success and I was determined no matter what happened, I would not ignore my family. By this time, it was very clear to me that this 'innocent-looking girl' was not genuine. However, I would never show any unhappiness about the marriage to my family.

Time passed between work and home, visiting both houses and various friends and relatives. Wherever possible, I took Suramya to historical places in the locality. When we were in Maduru-Oya, Suramya became pregnant and I brought her to her mother's home in Udahagama. At the same time, I got a transfer to the Colombo head office. This was a coincidence. After checking a few houses through friends, I finally found a housing unit in Battaramulla that my friend Shehan's sister used to rent. We were planning to go there, but Daya *Aiya* and Chitra *Akka* insisted we stay with them at their house, which was close to my office. I told Suramya to thank them for the offer, but that we would go to our own place, since we had more than enough furniture and household goods, and we needed our independence. Chitra *Akka*'s immediate younger brother Perakum was living at their house, and his office was also close by. Suramya told me Daya *Aiya* insisted we stay with them and otherwise they might get hurt. Daya *Aiya* has arranged Perakum's room for us and Perakum had shifted to the children's room. Finally, I agreed, and we went to live with Daya *Aiya*'s family. A few weeks went by happily, but Suramya started her habit of 'torturing the husband' again. After work, I came home happy to be with my pregnant wife, but most of the time, she had an angry face. I felt guilty staying there without any contribution, either sharing rent or paying for food. Chitra *Akka* kept a domestic servant for cooking and housecleaning. I suggested to Suramya rather than paying money, we may do the grocery shopping, to which she agreed. One day, we went to the nearby weekend market and bought a few bags of vegetables to start with. Chitra *Akka* was unhappy about this, and she told Daya *Aiya* so. They eventually told us not to bring anything, as they were completely happy to look after us, and it was not a burden.

Time slowly passed, and it was the right time to take Suramya to a gynaecologist for a check-up. I took her to a famous doctor, who was at the time retired but seeing patients at his residence. I felt very sorry for Suramya as the first question she asked was, 'Doctor, if it is a girl that I have conceived, will she get my skin?' This showed how much she had suffered from her own mother, when her mother told her she would never get married because of her rough skin. This had deeply embedded in Suramya's mind, and she was now worried about it. The kind doctor, like a father talking to a daughter, said, 'You don't have to worry about it. Even if she gets rough skin, there is nothing wrong with it – now you have married and are expecting a baby.' This helped to console Suramya, and she was very happy with the doctor and that I took her to him for the consultation.

To keep Suramya happy, at least a couple of days a week after work, I took her to the Galle Face Green in Colombo. In the evening, many people went there to exercise or just to relax and enjoy the sea breeze. The footpath was along the coast, and we would walk until Suramya had enough. Sometimes we ended up eating fish and chips from the mobile truck, which was parked in the Galle Road car park. Other days, we would go to Kollupitiya Chinese restaurant for dinner – our favourite was fried rice with chilli crabs or prawns. No matter what I did to keep her happy, her verbal abuse towards me never stopped. Some days it continued all night, making me tired and exhausted the following morning, and I would go to the office with swollen eyes. It appeared there was no end to this, and when there was nothing else to do, I suggested that maybe we should divorce and I would look after the baby. She declined, as it would bring a bad name to her family.

It surprised me Daya *Aiya* and Chitra *Akka* had never said a word, even though they had seen all the grumbling and rough treatment – perhaps because they didn't want to interfere. As the torture continued, and I saw no escape, I felt like committing suicide. One morning, after a sleepless night, I went to Suramya and put my hands together as if worshipping and begged her: 'Please don't do this to me. I am an innocent man. If I die, there is no one to look after my mother. I would like to see my child – please don't do this again.' I had no option and no shame; it was a matter of life and death. Suramya was sitting on the bed, looking at the wall in front of her. She never uttered a word. It was early in the morning, and I heard Chitra *Akka* making tea. I had not slept the night before, as Suramya's quarrel went on throughout the night. I couldn't help it; there was nothing to lose, so I shouted: 'Chitra *Akka* please come and helped me ... ask Suramya not to torture me.' She called Daya *Aiya* who was in their bedroom. They came to the room together and Daya *Aiya* spoke directly to Suramya: 'What has happened to you? We have noticed you grumble almost every day. At least give him a chance to sleep; he must go to work. Why can't you talk and sort something out? If you have a problem, you may talk to us.'

To this Suramya answered: 'He smokes.' I had nothing to say.

One day my good friend Kithsiri, who was working on a site, visited the head office. He invited me for a cup of tea at the nearby canteen. While we were sipping tea, Kithsiri said the guys in the office were talking about you, that you did not talk much and was always on your own, not moving with anyone.

'Are there any problems bothering you?' Kithsiri said. 'You must be open with me because we have been good friends for so long. I know that you have a marriage problem.'

I admitted it and briefly told him how Suramya treated me. After a lot of talking, Kithsiri made me promise I would not talk with anyone, especially with Suramya, about what we discussed.

'I am saying this only to tell you what is really going on,' Kithsiri said. It seemed his wife was a classmate of Suramya and a good friend. Kithsiri said he and his wife had spent a lot of time discussing whether to tell Senevi and finally decided they should.

'What are you talking about?' I said.

'You know Suramya had a boyfriend, don't you?' he asked.

I told him that was so long ago, during her school years, and that it was common among school children, though I personally did not have that experience.

'No, Senevi, that is not correct. That is what you have been told. The affair started during her high school days but continued until close to your marriage. Her mother opposed marrying Wickrama simply because she did not want to marry from the same family.'

I couldn't believe this; this is not what I had heard from her.

'That's not even the worst thing,' Kithsiri said. 'Senevi, we couldn't believe it when we heard this, and we felt very sorry for you. Others felt the same, and we thought of telling you to take care.'

'What is it?' I asked.

Kithsiri made me promise once again not to talk with anyone and particularly Suramya and not to get into an argument or enact any revenge, since she was now a pregnant woman. I promised and asked again, 'What is it?'

For a moment, he was silent and then slowly told me. Suramya had told her close friend that she married Senevi to get revenge on Wickrama. Not for any other reason. She had been asking Wickrama to marry her and take her away from her mother, but he did not do it because it would cause problems for his sister's marriage. As Wickrama was not giving confirmation of their marriage, Suramya became angry and decided to get revenge. She just wanted to show him, 'If a police officer cannot marry me, I will show that I can marry an engineer even.' That was all she wanted. That was the reason.

At that moment, my whole world collapsed; whatever hope left for living was gone and tears filled my eyes.

'Suramya's friend couldn't believe it; she told a couple of her friends and my wife was one of them,' said Kithsiri. I raised my head and asked who Suramya's friend was. He said he couldn't tell me her name, but all indications were that it was Priyani.

After Suramya's marriage, Wickrama had started to drink more alcohol, more frequently. Suramya heard all the news about him from her friend. Wickrama didn't attend the wedding and never visited their Udahagama house after her marriage. Cunningly,

Suramya's mother told me a couple of times: 'You know that Chitra has another brother in the police force. He used to visit us frequently, but now he never comes. I do not know why?' It appeared everyone had a hidden story behind the wedding they were still trying to hide from me. On one occasion, Nelum, was there when Suramya's mother said that, and she bent down towards her ear and told her in a low voice, 'He knows that.'

It was now very clear Suramya was making trouble for me not because I smoked, but because of her own wrongdoing not marrying her lover, or at least not remaining single. It was not a simple school children's love, apparently. Wickrama had decided to remain single. I felt I was the worst fool that ever lived in this world. I was sure, if my poor mother and sisters knew what suffering I was going through, they would die. I pretended all the time that I was having a happy life, just to keep them happy.

The following weekend, we went home. On Saturday we stayed at our home and later in the evening went to the Udahagama house. As usual, Nandimitra came in the evening, and we went to Kandy for a drink at their usual place in Colombo Street. After a few drinks, I told Nandimitra the story I heard from my friend. He didn't deny anything; instead he told me that Wickrama was the best person in that family, that he had very good qualities. But their mother opposed the marriage, so Wickrama took a step back, not giving a definite word, a kind of delaying tactic though he still loving Suramya. He did not want to marry her without the mother's blessing because his sister, Chitra, would have to pay for that. The mother was already giving enough trouble to Chitra. Nandimitra told me that he would speak to Suramya, but it seemed this never happened as she did not change.

Time passed by as usual. One day after work, when I came home, I saw Wickrama was playing with little Nandana and Nandani. One of Wickrama's arm was plastered. As I stepped into the lounge, I said hello and asked him what had happened.

'I met with an accident and came to stay with Chitra *Akka* for a few days,' he replied.

'That is good, you can play with Nandana and Nandani,' I said and went to our room, where Suramya was sitting on the bed.

'I did not know that he would come today and stay here,' she said. I told her that it would be very embarrassing for me to stay here and suggested, 'Let us go home for two weeks. I can come to work from home.' She refused, saying Daya *Aiya* may question why and cannot hurt him.

'We can say my mother is not so well and we need to stay at home,' I said, but again she refused, saying she could not hurt Daya *Aiya*. This was one of her favourite excuses. Obviously, Suramya might have wanted to talk to Wickrama personally or something more. When all the males, Daya *Aiya*, Perakum and I, would go to work in the morning, only Wickrama, Suramya and Chitra *Akka* would be left in the house. Suramya said she would stay in the room until I came home after work. Obviously, there was no need and one could not realistically do that. One need not do that, if one's mind was clear. So we stayed … and I lived with unbearable pain. She simply stayed there to look after him and convince him to stop drinking and marry. It was a well-kept family secret: only Suramya and Chitra *Akka* know what happened under that roof.

If you love someone, don't marry anyone else;
in this way four lives can be saved.

-Nara Somaratne-

Chapter 5

Pleasure of fatherhood and responsibilities

Time passed without any changes to our lives. Suramya was close to six months pregnant and wanted to go to her mother's place in Udahagama. This was the prevailing custom in Sri Lanka. We managed to find a kind female obstetrician–gynaecologist in Kandy, and I took Suramya for her regular check-ups. I left Daya *Aiya*'s house and went to stay with my sister in Kotte. On weekends, I went home to stay with Suramya to attend to her needs and we shopped for the baby in advance. We knew it was a boy and everyone in the family was excited and happy, particularly my family as there were no male descendants in the family. This was also a Sri Lankan tradition to expect male hierarchy in the family line.

The day finally arrived, and our sweet little son was born. I absorbed all the mental agony and pain of the past with Suramya to see this little son, and I was utterly thrilled. The feeling of being a father made me overwhelmed. Here was a son to call me *Appachchi* (father). We named him Tirath. Sugandhika was excited, and almost every day after school, she came to stay with Tirath, saying *Ukkun Malli* (meaning sweet little brother). I went home and brought my mother to see her grandson. Tears fell from her eyes and ran down her cheeks due to her extreme excitement and joy.

The first few weeks were very busy as everyone we knew, relatives and friends, visited to see our son. Suramya became a very busy woman. She never gave away any of the work, be it changing nappies, washing nappies, feeding our son, putting him to sleep – she did it by herself. She proved to be a good housewife; laziness was not in her vocabulary. My sisters saw this and often discussed how she managed it all by herself. Everyone at our place loved her. They often compared her to our Punchi *Akka,* who lived in Alawwa.

About two months after Tirath was born, I came home for the weekend and Suramya was unhappy. I asked her what had happened, and she said her mother had started to tell people who visited her home that she could not go to temple or meditation because of her daughter's child. Suramya said that her mother didn't do anything anyway, and even so, Suramya was not someone who would let someone else look after her child. With tears in her eyes, she said that what her mother indirectly was saying was to get out of her house. It was typical after childbirth for mothers to look after their daughters for at least three months or even longer. Suramya knew this and said her mother always mistreated her and that she just kept her there for a period merely to show the rest of the world. She was now talking about meditation and going to temples, but the truth was she never did that regularly. Suramya felt shamed and angry.

Finally, my younger sister Kumari managed to find an annexure in Nugegoda, which was part of a large house occupied by her manager. It was a small one-bedroom unit with a kitchen and bathroom. The dining area was reasonably large. We kept a second bed by the side of the dining table so that, if any visitor come, we had a second bed. I felt sorry as I could not afford Suramya a more spacious house. Through her contacts, Punchi *Akka* managed to find a domestic helper from the Kegalle area. The most important job she had to do was to stay near the child, while Suramya did the cooking, fed the child and washed clothes. Only minor works such as cleaning the house were given to the domestic helper.

All our siblings came to see us. Once Sugandhika came and stayed for a couple of weeks and we looked after her like our own child. Daya *Aiya* and his family were frequent visitors, and it was very nice to have them. The house owner's family were kind and friendly. Mr Padmasiri, my sister's manager, was from down south. His wife, Olga, was a teacher and a kind lady and her mother also lived with them; we called her 'aunty.' Padmasiri and Olga had a little daughter who sometimes came to our part of the house to play with Tirath. Sometimes we used to lay a mat outside the house in the garden and keep the child there, so he could roll over on the mat. I took public transport to the office and came home at midday for lunch. After work, I would sometimes go to Nugegoda market to do the grocery shopping, mainly vegetables.

Once a month on weekends we went home and when we returned, we brought rice, coconut and vegetables, given to us by our families. On our way back, we would stop to buy local fruits, usually sweet pineapples, for ourselves and for Daya *Aiya*'s family and my sister Seela, who lived in Kotte. It was a lovely time – though we were not rich, we could manage with my salary, and we were happy. As my younger sister Kumari was also working, she shared the family responsibilities. This did not mean that I was relieved of my duties, though. I still had a lot to do to raise the living standards of my family, siblings and their children, to provide the children with a good education and to help them build their houses. I understood, with my salary, this childhood dream could not be achieved.

After coming to the Colombo office, new possibilities were opening up in terms of life direction. Overseas employment opportunities, particularly to the Middle East, with attractive salary packages for engineers, were becoming available. Some of my friends had already taken offers and left for work overseas. Another attractive option was to get a higher study scholarship for post-graduate studies, particularly in the US, Canada or Australia. For this to happen, some postgraduate studies were needed in addition to experience. Coincidently, there was a postgraduate course about to start at my former university, the University of Moratuwa and some of my colleague has already enrolled. I also applied and enrolled, and my employer offered two days per week of study leave for a year. So, I began a new life as a student again. Our family life was as usual; not much changed, though little Tirath was growing up. We had some friends nearby, and whenever we had time, we visited them or they visited us. Other frequent visitors were my sisters' and Daya *Aiya*'s families.

A year later, I graduated with a Postgraduate Diploma in Land and Water Management. It was a great relief – I could now apply for overseas universities. According to colleagues, the US and Australia offered great opportunities. I obtained memberships of the Institute of Engineers in each country as this recognition was vital. I got admitted to several universities, but no financial assistance was offered, meaning either I must pay on my own or continue to earn after entering university by doing part-time work. Many friends and colleagues suggested Australia offered better flexibility in terms of part-time work and study. The plan was to go overseas for two years, complete a Master's degree part-time and then come back to Sri Lanka.

We told Daya *Aiya* this idea the next time we saw him. To our surprise, about two or three months later, we got a sponsoring letter from Suramya's brother, Kumara, who was living in Adelaide at the time. When we asked him how this occurred, Daya *Aiya* told us he had spoken to Kumara, and asked him to sponsor us, as it would expedite the process for us. Within a few months of submitting the relevant documents, we were granted immigration visas. At the interview, the immigration officer told me that acceptance by the Australian Institute of Engineers provided proof of qualifications, and that it would be easy to find a job now.

This was our first overseas travel, and we were enthusiastically dreaming about working and living in Australia for at least two years before returning to Sri Lanka. But before going to Australia, there were some things to take care of. I asked Sudu *Akka* to return home and stay with Amma for two years up until I returned, then I sold my car and put some funds in Sudu *Akka*'s account.

About two weeks before our departure to Australia, we were at Suramya's place in Udahagama. Mid-morning, I heard loud voices and when I went to see what the commotion was, I saw it was Suramya and her mother arguing in the dining room. Not knowing what was going on, I moved to the lounge-room area. They were shouting at each other, growling like two tigers fighting in a forest. In the middle of this, Nandimitra arrived. I went to the veranda outside and Nandimitra said, with great embarrassment, he had seen this many times before and not to go and ask them what it was about. I told Nandimitra I had not seen this level of fighting between a mother and daughter before, not even in the neighbourhood we lived in, which was a colony. I said, '*Aiya*, I'm not going to Australia. I don't have anyone there. At least my siblings, relatives and friends are here. Going to an unknown country with this woman is certain to cause misery.'

'Please don't do that *Malli*,' Nandimitra answered. 'Everything is arranged, and you have resigned from your job. Therefore, please go as planned. In a new environment, she may not behave as she is doing here.' I had my doubts, but I agreed to go to Australia, anyway.

Everything will be okay in the end.
If it's not okay, it's not the end.

-John Lennon-

Chapter 6

Life in Australia

On 26th September 1986, a day before Tirath's birthday, we arrived in Adelaide. Daya *Aiya* had booked Singapore Airlines with two days' stopover in Singapore. We walked around the area close to the hotel. I carried Tirath the whole time as he was crying all the way from Colombo to Singapore and while we were walking around the streets. Later we realised he was hungry but refusing to drink pasteurised bottled milk as he was used to powdered milk in Sri Lanka.

When we landed in Adelaide, I was very excited to come out of the airport and see the landscape and environment. Kumara had come to the airport to welcome us and take us to his home in Warradale. We only had two suitcases and were carrying about 2000 dollars in cash. When we arrived at Kumara's house, his wife Mina welcomed us. She was very happy as they now had family in Australia. They both cuddled little Tirath, who ran around the house and garden. The following day was a Saturday and Tirath's second birthday, and Kumara and Mina helped us celebrate, cutting a small cake and giving him presents.

The following week was very busy. Kumara took us to register as newly arrived unemployed at the Centrelink office, and to open up a bank account and get private medical insurance for which he paid the first few month's premium. Kumara and Mina took us out for lunch and dinner to places such as KFC and Pizza Hut, as we had never tasted them before. Little Tirath was overjoyed to eat outdoors. Kumara was helpful in getting us settled. Almost every evening, he would sit with us and talk about life in Australia. He asked us not to withdraw money from our account and even told me to smoke cigarettes from his cartons. Both Kumara and Mina were smokers. Both Kumara and Mina worked at different places, and they mostly took public transport to work. Kumara would give Suramya 50 dollars on his payday.

A few days after arriving in Adelaide, Suramya started her old game again. For no reason, she started to quarrel and sometimes during the night she would cry to get the attention of her brother. This was her tactic. She used tears to get attention and sympathy, which was very frustrating. Instead of helping or encouraging her husband to find work, she made trouble. When asked 'why you are doing this?' her only regular answer was, 'you are smoking.' What she really wanted, as she did in Sri Lanka, was to show her brothers strength and to dominate me. Day after day, this happened; it had become part of my life. I was in a miserable situation with no friend or relatives living in Adelaide.

One day, she quarrelled through the night. In the morning, I was outside the house in the backyard and saw Suramya coming towards the screen door carrying some washing in a basket. To help her, I opened the screen door and held it for her. As she came past, she hit the left side of my upper rib cage with her elbow. For a minute, I could not breathe and it was painful. Kumara was sitting at the second dining table next to the back door and he saw what happened. He rushed over and shouted at Suramya: 'What did you do that for? Why all this? I have been watching what you are doing these last few months, and **the way you torture your husband is far worse than what our mother did to our father**.

'Both Dayananda and Nandimitra told me all about you,' he continued. 'You could not stay with mother without quarrelling; now you cannot stay with your husband without quarrelling. You do not know how to live with other people as you have not been in the workforce.' That night I could not sleep. I was thinking about what had happened to me to undergo this suffering. It was all revealed now why her father used to work in distant places and only came to Kandy close to his retirement. Where could I go? Nowhere. I had to stay with her to raise Tirath. Was this going to be my life? Had she learned this habit from her mother, or was it part of her heritage, this 'fix your husband the way you want' attitude her mother had taught her? Was I born to undergo this suffering? I felt like leaving and going wherever I liked, just to escape from her. But where could I go? Nowhere. I was alone. Suramya was showing her power. She did this at Dayananda's house and now it had started again. Here was I, struggling to establish a new life, and rather than giving support or at least encouraging me, she wanted to continue torturing me.

After a few quiet days, Suramya started nagging again. I had a responsibility to raise a child, because of that I had to live with her. Little Tirath was the only solace. After this incident, I was determined to respond immediately; if she threw me one line, I would throw two lines back at her and respond appropriately. I would stop her shouting at me with whatever force I could use. But at Kumara's house I couldn't do it because I was a guest of her brother.

One of the most useful pieces of advice Kumara gave me was that as soon as I got a job, I should save for a house deposit. Buying a house is an Australian dream, he said. This advice settled deeply within me. I prepared several versions of my CV, written in Sri Lankan style, and with no Australian referees on it. The standard of the CV was poor, and most employers did not even acknowledge receipt. Kumara said I should feel free to ring local companies and make inquiries about any vacancies. When he returned home after work, he would ask how the job hunting was going. One day, a construction company responded. The company director said he required a site engineer at their Centennial Park construction site, but he could only afford a trade person's salary of about 400 dollars a week. I was thrilled and everyone was very happy. It was a good starting point.

For the first few weeks, Kumara gave me his car for me to go to work. Some days, the company director drove past and picked me up and dropped me off after work. Eventually, I bought an old Nissan Sunbird from a co-worker on the site. Now that we had a car, we could go out on weekends with Tirath to his favourite places, such as Glenelg Beach. Tirath would run after seagulls in the park. We would have lunch outside – fish or chicken with chips. Tirath also liked ice creams. We took him several times to the Adelaide Zoo and Cleland Wildlife Park.

One day, Suramya told me we should look for a house to rent and it was time for us to go. I asked her why she suddenly wanted to leave. Suramya said she had seen an unfinished letter of Mina to her cousin, which said, 'It is interesting to have a large family, but our freedom is now limited.' Before I could remind her it was disgusting to read other people's letters, Suramya said, 'I know it is bad to read, but I wanted to know what they think about us.'

Not needing another reason to quarrel, I started to search for a small affordable unit in Ascot Park. Once it was ready, I told

Kumara we were going to live in a separate house. He became angry and asked why we were leaving in such a hurry. 'At least you should have told me before,' he said. 'If you stayed here, you could build up your savings, and that is why I asked you to stay with us.'

However, we moved to the Ascot Park anyway, and the time we spent there was interesting. Suramya took Tirath to the nearby play school. Suramya had the opportunity to meet other ladies who brought their kids there and made some new friends. Tirath was very interesting, and we eagerly watched American wrestling fights together on TV. Sometimes he fought with me, and I pretended I was losing and fell on the ground. Then he walked around and showed his tiny fist to his mother and proudly said, 'Did you see that? I can even kick him out.' Whenever there were wildlife documentaries on, we eagerly watched them together. Tirath was very keen on watching animals, any animals. Sometimes, he crawled like tigers or lions. It made me think one day he would become a zookeeper. One of his favourite movies was *Hatari!*. He even acted like 'Pockets' (Red Buttons) and Sean Mercer (John Wayne). Tirath was also very talkative and liked to hear about my childhood in Huruluwewa, about the things I did, walking through the forest and rice fields, and bird watching. I bought him a book on Australian animals, and read to him about spiders, snakes and birds which he listened to eagerly.

A few weeks after shifting to the new place, the construction site was closed, as almost all the work had been completed. Various tradesmen found work elsewhere in the building industry, but I did not have the opportunity. One day, a tradesman told me he was joining a construction company laying sewer pipes in the Adelaide Hills. He said he could talk to the company owner and get me a labourer's job. I agreed and started to work as a labourer, just to earn a few more dollars to support the family. The job was to backfill trenches after laying sewer pipes. This was one of the hardest manual jobs I have ever done, sometimes in muddy conditions after rain, other times working in soggy filthy conditions because of a leaking septic tank effluent. A thousand times I thought, what happened to my career as a 'chartered civil engineer'? This was not what I expected or deserved. However, during this time, with additional savings, we managed to get a home loan and bought a house in Hackham East, close to the kindergarten. The company owner gave me a letter guaranteeing my job. We moved to a new place and informed Kumara, who was in Perth that year. He was very happy I had followed his advice. During their absence, Suramya made no trouble.

When it was the right time, Tirath was admitted to pre-school. The first day of his schooling, I stayed home, and we took him to the teacher and introduced him. When we returned home, we felt lonely without Tirath and wondered whether he was crying without his parents. So we returned and stayed behind the gum tree in front of the pre-school and watched. Sometimes Tirath would go to the sandpit with other children, stay a few minutes and come to the gate, probably to check whether his parents were still there. Sometimes he walked around the front garden alone. When he came home that afternoon, he was chattering normally and seemed happy. We thought we must speak in English so that he would pick up the language easily and that would help him to get on with other children. However, his teacher visited us for a cup of tea one day and said not to speak at home in English as he would soon pick it up. Being able to speak two languages would be more useful for his future development.

Day by day Tirath was growing. We took him to the nearby park to use the swings, ladders and slippery dip. Initially, he was afraid to go on the slippery dip, but I took him on my lap and went down until his fear went away. Both Suramya and Tirath had new friends. Suramya's old friend Debbie visited occasionally with her children. Our next-door neighbours Paul and Kay had two lovely children and Tirath sometimes got together and played with them. Out the front of our house lived a lovely old couple, and the man told Tirath to call him 'Pa' (grandpa). Gradually Tirath was becoming more knowledgeable about a clean environment and if he went out with us for a walk in the park or to the Noarlunga Centre, if he saw any litter thrown, he would pick it up and put it in the bin. He was growing up and becoming mature very fast and would sit with us to watch 'Andy Hardy' movies. He started to call me 'Sir,' instead of *Achchi* as Andy Hardy (Mickey Rooney) called his father, Judge Hardy. Tirath's knowledge of animals was ever expanding, and he knew about dinosaurs and reticulated pythons and anacondas. As any child of a similar age, he exaggerated things. One day he asked me how long did I think an anaconda was? When I said about six feet, he laughed and said, 'The length of a small anaconda is about from here (Hackham) to Christies Beach (about 8 kilometres long) and needs 16 people to carry it.' When we were going to Adelaide along the Main South Road, there was a small pocket of pine forest after Reynella, and Tirath would always ask us to keep silent because dinosaurs might be there. Day by day life became more interesting, and because of Tirath I felt it was worth living now, forgetting all the mistreatment from Suramya. Tirath came and worked in the backyard with me in the vegetable plot, with his never-ending chatter. Even if he stood or sat down, he followed the way I stood, keeping both hands in his pockets and sometimes with twisted legs.

After a year in Perth, Kumara and Mina returned to Adelaide and started to work in their old positions. Apparently, they had taken leave with no pay for one year. With the arrival of her brother, Suramya started her old habit again. One day, she began quarrelling for no apparent reason. When she was angry, no one could stop her arguing with a loud voice. I asked again and again, but it was no use. I could not counter-argue with her, and I used the only option available at the time – hitting her mouth and telling her, 'At least now you'll shut up.' As she turned her face away, my hand landed above the mouth, making a dark bruise near her right eye. This was the first time in my life that I had raised my hand to hit someone and I very much regretted it. Later in the week when we visited Kumara and Mina, Kumara said, 'It is an offence to hit your wife and you may be even go to jail.' My answer to him was simple: 'At least it would be better than living with this woman.' He didn't say anything more – probably because he himself had witnessed her rude behaviour when we were living in his house.

Towards the end of the work project, I decided that it was not a permanent way for us to live in Australia; either I must go back to Sri Lanka or study further to get a suitable position here that I deserved. One day, I went to the South Australian Institute of Technology (now University of South Australia) with a letter I had received from Monash University and met with the head of Civil Engineering and expressed my willingness to do a Master's degree. He promptly said, 'Prof. John Argue is looking for a research student,' and directed me to him. After a brief discussion about my university education and experience, Prof. Argue was quite happy to supervise me and did everything possible to admit me and start the research work. It was a one-year research project. After discussion with Social Security, Prof. Argue arranged fortnightly payments for me for the duration. He also arranged to get supplementary payments working for the university research contract projects. As the project duration was one year, I had to work hard, mainly doing experimental works in daytime and data analysis during night-time. Periodically, I worked three-day cycles of day-night work, and that meant little time left for Tirath. Sometimes, he would knock on the door and when I asked him what he wanted, his almost certain answer was 'shall we have a little chat?' I would ask, 'What about?' and his usual answer was 'about animals.' He would initially sit on my lap, and then climb onto the table and sit comfortably. Besides keeping up the study work, I spent time with Tirath, which we both enjoyed.

Suramya and Tirath would take the bus to the Noarlunga Library to borrow books and buy small grocery items. Suramya told me one day when walking along the corridor near the butcher's shop, Tirath had said, '*Amma*, when *Achchi* gets a job, can we buy that meat and fry it and eat it?' On hearing this, my eyes became wet. Even at a small age, he never asked anything, made no trouble for his parents, and showed every sign of being a perfect boy. It reminded me of my own childhood and teen years.

Christmas in 1988 was special. At the university, John asked me the address of my home in Hackham and what a surprise, on 24th December, he knocked on the door with a large esky and some clothes and toys for Tirath. John said he and his wife Anne did some Christmas shopping for us and unpacked the esky and went away wishing us 'Merry Christmas and a happy new year for 1989.' He had brought us rice, lentils, dried fruits, chicken and cakes. Thereafter, Tirath called him 'Santa Claus,' as John had a long white beard and had brought us Christmas presents.

Time slowly passed, and I graduated in 1989. One day, John called me into his office and asked what I was going to do now. I told him I was looking for a job in government or in a consultancy company. He advised me not to go straight to consulting companies even though they paid a small amount more than the government. He asked to see my CV and revised, re-typed and kept a copy with him, advising me to apply for a research hydrology position advertised in the Department of Agriculture. Several weeks later, I received the acknowledgement letter advising I had been shortlisted for an interview. Following an intense interview process, I was selected and offered the position. Immediately, I informed John and thanked him for his effort, and in return he wished me well in the new job. Jay, who had been educated in agricultural engineering in the US, was the section head in charge of the department. He was very friendly and one day he told me that John had rung him frequently to ask about my progress throughout the selection process.

Now I had a stable job and our family life gradually improved. We could afford new clothes and good food. We started saving for the future and even made a trip back to Sri Lanka for a holiday. The work was challenging as I had to do some experimental work as well as developing a mathematical model for water infiltration through soil surface. Apart from working in the office, I spent time working at home to achieve progress as it was a new project and everyone expected a lot from me. Jay was impressed with the progress achieved towards broad departmental goals. One day, Jay told me he had been talking about me with Peter, the CSIRO's director of the newly established Centre for Groundwater Studies, and he was very keen to meet me. Jay suggested I continue the project towards a PhD and asked me to write a proposal.

After reviewing the proposal, Peter took me to meet the Dean of the Faculty of Earth Sciences at Flinders University. After a lengthy discussion, I was told that subject area was well worthy of a PhD and the Dean was willing to admit me as a PhD student supervised by both the university and the CSIRO. He also advised me jokingly not to talk much about this opportunity at my workplace, as most of my colleagues would be jealous. Further, he said that what I had was a very rare opportunity – working full time as an employee and becoming a full-time student. I was determined to complete the research work to the best of my ability, and CSIRO also provided more facilities at their soil physics laboratory to conduct further experiments. Once again, I was a student.

By this time Suramya was pregnant again and this time it was a girl. We informed both families in Sri Lanka who were very happy and only worried there was no help for Suramya, as typically was the case in Sri Lanka. We both managed it all. Suramya was not the type of woman to easily get tired. House cleaning, cooking and washing continued as usual. I, of course, tended to the work outside, mainly the garden. Tirath was very excited about having a little sister. Suramya told him about taking care of his little sister. As he accompanied his mother to the clinic for check-ups, he also listened to her tummy and said his sister talked to him. He made the noise of lungs working exactly as they do, and it was a fun for him to listen to. Whenever we had a break, we would pick strawberries at nearby farms, go to Christies Beach or just have a little drive in the countryside. The good thing was that, in this pregnancy, Suramya did not become wild; perhaps she might have understood, or she might have thought that there was no one around other than me. Tirath was told, in an emergency, to ring triple zero and tell them that 'my mother is going to have a baby, there is no one at home, we need an ambulance.' He practised this well, and we were confident that he would do that if the need arose.

By this time, Jay was planning to go to Sydney to lead a groundwater modelling group in the NSW Department of Water Resources. He was taking one year's leave without pay. I had by then completed the mathematical model and was in the process of validating with laboratory and field data. The new head of the section, Steve, a quiet gentleman, was very supportive. He had been overseas on a consultancy mission and had just returned. As soon as Jay went to Sydney, he telephoned me at home and told me he was working with really good people some of whom were recognised as experts in groundwater. He said they had received a large amount of funds to develop several groundwater models, some of them the largest in Australia. Further, he would soon create and advertise a senior groundwater modelling position. At the same time, my CSIRO supervisor said that he would be going to a laboratory in Townsville and asked me to keep in contact with him. By this time, we had published research outcomes in several conference papers, and he encouraged me to write a journal article, which I did. What remained was to write the thesis.

Close to the delivery, Kumara sponsored his mother for a holiday. She stayed with Kumara, but came to visit us with them. All my family members in Sri Lanka were happy as Suramya's mother was visiting. For the delivery, I took Suramya to the private hospital and her mother came to stay with us. One day, after the hospital visit, I bought a bottle of wine and started to drink it while cooking dinner. Suddenly, she shouted at me. I asked her why she was shouting.

'You are drinking wine!' she said.

'So, what?' was my reply.

'When children do wrong things, mothers need to correct them!' she said, firing up.

'You are not my mother, but mother-in-law,' I responded. 'And how many of your sons drink and smoke? More than me, almost every day. Why don't you go and correct them?' I said angrily, loud and clear, then adding, 'Suramya used to kill me every day as you told her to "fix your husband the way you want." There is nothing wrong to fix here – and did you ask your daughters-in-law to fix their husbands – your three sons?'

This had been on my mind for years, and at least I could tell her now.

'I am leaving,' she said.

'Go away, and do not come again,' I told her.

She telephoned Kumara and asked him to come and picked her up. In no time, he came to the door and took her back to his place.

A couple of hours later, Suramya telephoned; she was crying, and she asked me what had happened. I told her everything. Suramya said her mother telephoned her at the hospital, abused her and told her that 'we are going to chase you out of our family.' I felt very sorry for her – a mother abusing her daughter when she was about to give birth – it was very strange. Suramya said her mother wouldn't have known the hospital number, so she was certain Kumara had made the call and told her mother to abuse her. It was disgusting, being a woman, a mother herself, and abusing her daughter without even considering her situation. Suramya suspected it was a planned incident.

Two days later was the delivery day. Tirath and I went to the hospital to see Suramya. As it was a paid ward, there were no restrictions. We stayed near her while she was in labour, but because of the pain, she could not talk much. Two nurses were with her, and close to the delivery, one of them asked me if I wanted to stay. I said I would love to, but I couldn't because Tirath may get scared. He was already upset seeing his mother's tears. I took him out of the delivery room and the nurse told us to come back in two hours' time. We did not go far. I bought hot chips for Tirath's lunch, and we sat on the steps at the back-door area of the hospital. Everything that had happened was on my mind. There was no one in Adelaide we knew – no relatives and friends. The three of us were alone, soon to become four …

We went back to the maternity ward at the designated time. There she was wrapped in a warm blanket having a nice nap. A sweet, little bubbly girl with a red face. Suramya was relieved and smiling. She told us after the baby was cleaned, they gave her to Suramya for breastfeeding and then she slept. We stayed for about an hour looking at the little girl and then went home to arrange the house.

The day she came home was a very hot day, about 40°C degrees. There was no air conditioning in the old car. To our surprise, the baby did not cry; she slept all the way home. We named her Kumudu. Little Tirath was very helpful to his mother. Suramya got him involved, so the bond between them would become strong. We informed our family and particularly my mother about the girl. Without knowing anything that had happened, they once again said it was nice Suramya's mother was with her during the needy hour. We decided not to tell anyone, but apparently Kumara had telephoned Dayananda and talked about it – obviously his version.

After everything settled, I started to go back to the office. Gradually, our lives began to return to normal. Suramya took Tirath to school with Kumudu in a baby sling. Our next-door neighbour Kay and Suramya used to go to school together. Little Kumudu never cried even if she got wet nappies or pooed.

Three weeks later, Suramya telephoned me in the office and asked me to come home, as there was sad news from Sri Lanka.

'Is it about *Amma*?' I said.

'Yes, she has died of a heart attack,' said Suramya.

I applied for a few days' leave and hurried home. We telephoned the Kurunegala home with tears in our eyes. They explained the funeral arrangements and asked me to come home to attend the funeral. I explained that I couldn't leave Suramya, as she was helpless with a little baby. It was a sad incident. Later on, my sister Kumari sent us the videotape of the funeral, with some clothes for Tirath and Kumudu.

Lots of things happened that year, in 1990. In January, Kumudu was born and then my mother died, and now the interest rate of our home loan had gone from 9% to 17.5%. In the meantime, Sudu *Akka* had sent a letter saying it was high time for me to come back to Sri Lanka, and she could look after me and my family. It was difficult making a decision. I was in Australia, and out of those two years, I had no savings beyond day-to-day living expenses. I completely understood Sudu *Akka*'s concern, and I had a big responsibility to look after them, plus still my younger sister had not married. This had to be arranged as she had never had any acquaintances or a boyfriend. I said to Sudu *Akka*, if an opportunity came for an arranged marriage, to give the Kurunegala house for her.

Time passed slowly. Kumudu was growing up and walking around the house. She never cried and always had a lovely smile on her face. Tirath was ever-hungry for new knowledge, and we started to collect volumes of an encyclopedia, one by one. Tirath had a separate room next to ours. He was afraid of the dark, so when he walked from one room to another after dark, he would shout loudly. In May 1990, my sister Kumari visited us and stayed for six months. She enjoyed the time with the children and shared Tirath's room. We visited several interesting places with her, such as the Almond Blossom Festival in Willunga and Cleland National Park. Suramya was happy to have a sister at home.

Towards the end of the year, there was a rumour spread at work that the research fund would cease in 1991, and we were asked to write strong project proposals; otherwise, we would lose our positions. This created a strong uncertainty in the work environment and was a hot topic amongst colleagues. On the other hand, Jay had created a senior groundwater modelling position and requested I apply for it. The position was at a senior level and the salary was almost double. By this time, Suramya was pregnant again. My sister Kumari went back to Sri Lanka in November. I had to make a vital and critical decision within a short time. I telephoned Jay, and he told me he had already talked with his managers about me and about my mathematical programming skills and they were very happy to meet me. I applied for the position and Jay arranged an interview. I stayed an extra day in Paramatta to go through the types of works the hydrogeology team was doing. I also met a few Sri Lankans who were working in the department, and some of them were former colleagues of mine from Sri Lanka.

After talking with Suramya, we decided to take up the new position, which meant selling the house and moving to Sydney. After all, it was a permanent position so I would have job security. When Kumudu started to talk, she used to say, 'This is not our house. We have a big house and three nice cars.' When we asked her where the house was, she always said it was in a big garden. We thought maybe she was recalling a past life in which she had lived a happy life with a rich family, and probably the girl accidentally died. In any case, we kept this to ourselves, as we thought it might attract the media and other interested parties that might affect the child's life.

In January 1991, we moved to Sydney and started to work in the Department of Water Resources. Jay has arranged a house in Wentworthville for us to rent. Tirath enrolled in the Pendle Hill primary school. He was a keen student and his teacher used to call him 'Walking Encyclopedia,' as his general knowledge was marvellous. As a habit, when he got dressed to go to school, he randomly selected a page of the encyclopedia and read it. Once a salesman came to promote encyclopedias and described the advantage of having an encyclopedia at home as we had a growing family. Turning a few pages in his encyclopedia, he asked some knowledge testing questions from Tirath and amazingly Tirath answered very well. The salesman said, 'I am amazed at this child's knowledge; he does not need any encyclopedia!'

Jay and his wife Shahanaz had arranged a good obstetrician and gynaecologist, Dr Phillip, for Suramya. At the right time, Suramya was admitted to the Westmead Hospital as a private patient. I looked after Tirath and Kumudu at home. Kumudu was always with me wherever I went; she followed me around calling me '*Achchi*.' During the night, I kept them in our bed, and we slept together. One day I received a telephone call from Suramya and she said, 'You wanted to have a cheeky boy – he's here now.' On 13th March, little Sirimath was born. The following morning, I took Tirath and Kumudu to the hospital. Tirath was such a sensitive child – he told me '*Achchi,* we have to take some flowers for *Amma*.' I really appreciated Tirath's thoughtfulness.

Daya *Aiya* had told some friends of his who were living in Sydney that we had moved there, and they visited us. One day when I was in the queue for renewing my drivers' license, I met a pleasant person Gamini, who asked me whether I was a new immigrant. I said I had come from Adelaide and was living in Wentworthville. Gamini and family also lived in the same suburb, but close to Westmead. We were on the other end, close to Pendle Hill. He invited us to visit his place, and we eventually did. Gamini, his wife Lali and three children lived in a recently built townhouse. The house we rented was a renovated old home. Gamini and his wife, Lali, were from down south in Sri Lanka, a town called Ambalangoda. They introduced us to their Sri Lankan GP, who made home visits. On one of the home visits, the GP said that the house was large with high ceilings and therefore would not be easy to keep warm during the winter. He suggested, if possible, that we should move to a newer and smaller place.

Later on, Gamini said one of the town house in their complex had become vacant. So we shifted to Wentworth St to a recently completed townhouse. The location was excellent as it was within walking distance of the railway station and close to the primary school. The house was facing the railway line, and it had become a habit of little Sirimath to watch the trains. By the sound of the train, he knew whether it was a small suburban or long interstate train. Such an intelligent little chap. Accordingly, he used to go to either the kitchen for the former or the upstairs bedroom for the latter.

In front of the house, there was a large gum tree, which I would park the car under. We enrolled Tirath at Westmead primary school. Suramya would push the stroller with the two little children in it to drop Tirath off at school every morning, and the same to pick him up after school. Suramya was scared to drive in Australia, though she had a Sri Lankan drivers' license. With repeated convincing, she agreed to take driving lessons and finally got her license, which was convenient and she enjoyed driving around, but not too far, only to the school, supermarket and Wentworthville library. By this point, due to my being overweight, poor eating habits and lack of exercise, combined with my family history, I was diagnosed as having elevated blood pressure and diabetes. I had been almost addicted to eating fried pork chops and smoked hocks.

Work was interesting and challenging. The primary responsibility was to develop the one of the largest groundwater models ever built in the Murray–Darling Basin: the Murrumbidgee basin model. The manager Mike and Jay were happy about the progress achieved. In addition to the main model, I had to develop a few other groundwater models in parallel. From morning to late evening, I worked, and this meant further delays to the completion of my thesis.

Our social life was also improving as we had quite a few Sri Lankan friends by then, and we made family visits whenever we could find time. There were a number of Sri Lankans working in the department, some of whom I had known back in Sri Lanka. One day I met Ranjith at the office who was undergoing work experience at the department. Ranjith and I had worked together in Sri Lanka. Ranjith was married to Chandrani, who was also from upcountry in Gampola. We visited each other and became good family friends. Chandrani was doing childcare work, looking after children at home as they did not have children at the time. We ourselves made a visit to Taronga Zoo, the Harbour Bridge and various other interesting places. Now both of us had Sri Lankan's friends to socialise with.

Once we settled in the new environment, and I got used to the responsibilities of the new position, I recommenced writing my thesis. Jay gave me permission to take the office laptop computer home, as I did not have my own computer. As Sirimath grew up, he started to run around the house. He would go to the kitchen and open the cupboards and get the cooking pans out and play. Once he cut his finger, another time he hit his head on the corner of the table and wounded himself. There was no walking with Sirimath, just running. Tirath started to call him 'Punky,' a nickname that lasted for years until he grew up to become a young man. On weekends, I normally worked at the dining table. Suramya would keep Sirimath in his playpen until she finished her housework, because it was much easier to get things done. Sometimes, Sirimath looked at me and called out 'oi' to get my attention. After a few repeats, I would go to him and take him out of the playpen and hold him on my lap for a while. Kumudu was growing and once, when she was walking down the steps, she fell and rolled down to the bottom and cried. Luckily, she was not hurt. Thereafter, she learned to sit on the steps and slowly descend, one by one. It was a most pleasant and memorable thing to watch her smiling face as she descended; it's never left my mind. It was lovely to see in the morning and a blessing for the day ahead. Tirath once again excelled in school at Westmead primary. By this time, he had become a good artist and one of his paintings was exhibited in the Sydney Museum and we all went to see it.

Once Daya *Aiya* and Chitra *Akka* came to Sydney. Daya *Aiya* had a training course and Chitra *Akka* stayed with us for the period. We took her around interesting places in Sydney. We did not have much money, but we were a little happy family.

One day Suramya told me she would also like to do childcare work at home, to which I agreed. She got all the necessary information from Chandrani. Firstly, she needed to do a course, which could be done as distant study. We paid the fee for the course. Suramya was highly experienced in childcare looking after her own children at home, so there was no doubt she deserved to pass the diploma, which she did. The problem was getting a job, which was difficult with two little children. It turned out she couldn't do childcare work from home as we did not have a dedicated room and other facilities. So she had to wait some time.

Suramya was the one who communicated with families in Sri Lanka. She never neglected to post birthday cards or new year cards to anyone on both sides of the family. Occasionally, we used to telephone home. One day, she told me she heard that Podi *Aiya* (Wickrama) got married to a lawyer. Her mother had attended the wedding and told her all about it. I had nothing to say; I just listened to her.

There were a number of Sri Lankans working in the department's regional offices as well. Whenever they came to the head office in Paramatta, they would visit people they knew in the office to maintain contact. We would phone them using the office phone. One such person was Lal, who went to the same school as me, but was not a classmate or batch mate, as he went to a different university. But we knew each other. Whenever Lal came to Sydney, he would stay with a friend to save the meal and accommodation allowance. This was a common practice, and everyone helped each other this way. One day, I met him in the corridor, and he said that on his next visit he would stay with me.

'Of course you can,' I said, and we exchanged a few more words and went to our respective floors. When he visited, he worked with the engineering team, where there were three of his batch mates: Piyal, Sunil and Siva. Siva was from the Sri Lankan Tamil community and he was Lal's batch mate. On another occasion, I met Lal at the office corridor at the entrance and after we exchanged a few greetings, he said he was going to stay with me that night. He had come to the office for routine work. I said 'yes,' and telephoned Suramya that a friend was coming to stay with us that night. On our way home, we stopped and went to the Wentworthville liquor shop to buy some alcohol: for me wine and, for Lal, a small bottle of whisky. Thereafter, I went to the butcher shop and bought a few slices of pork for dinner. As there was no additional room for a visitor, we arranged Kumudu and Sirimath's room for Lal to keep his clothes and change. We took the mattress downstairs for Lal to sleep, and I had a mat downstairs. Tirath had his room and Suramya said she would keep little Kumudu and Sirimath in our bedroom, as it had a double bed.

Lal was a pleasant person and told me he had two daughters. He was sitting on the second step of the staircase from the ground floor and playing a game with Kumudu. It was just hiding a small object in his hand behind him and asking Kumudu to guess which hand the object was in. He told me he loved to play with his daughters; sometimes they would take mother's nail polish and apply it; other times they would take lipstick and apply it on him and he said he loved it. I helped Suramya in the kitchen, slicing pork and frying. From time to time, we came out to see what the children and Lal were doing.

While the children were having their dinner, we enjoyed our drinks with a few pieces of fried pork. We were talking about our school days and various classmates who went into engineering degree courses. As the following day was a workday, after dinner we thought we would go to sleep, Lal on his mattress and I on the mat. Suramya and the children slept upstairs. I have a habit of falling into a deep sleep after I have had a drink. This was observed during my young days in Mahaweli. Sometimes, I even went to bed without dinner.

The following morning, when I woke up, Lal was sitting on the mattress. He said that he didn't have a good sleep as I was snoring heavily. After having a drink, it's true I snore loudly. After breakfast, we were ready to go to the office. I decided to take the car as it was school holiday time. I went to the car and was waiting for Lal to come. A few minutes later, he got into the car and closed the car door. At the very last minute, Suramya opened the front door and Lal said, 'I'll just go and say goodbye.' He jumped out of the car and went to the front door, and stood there talking and laughing for two or three minutes. This seemed strange to me, as what was there to talk about for two people who were completely unknown to each other until the previous evening? Even if he needed to say goodbye, it could have been done at the car as the car was parked just in front of the front door. After we arrived at the office, we went to our respective teams on different floors of the building.

Late one evening, Suramya told me two days before Lal had telephoned. I was surprised; why had he telephoned home when he used to call me in the office? How he knew the home phone number I did not know.

'What did he say?' I said. Suramya said he asked Senevi not to drink too much, and she laughed loudly. 'What else?' I asked.

'Nothing more,' she said. 'At the time Chandrani was also visiting.'

On another occasion, not too far from the first incident, we were watching a *Golden Years of Hollywood* movie presented by Bill Collins. Out of the blue, Suramya said, 'Hereafter when a friend visits, you don't have to sleep with them on the ground floor; you have to stay with us upstairs and let him sleep downstairs.' For no obvious reason, she said this in the middle of the movie, and my mind started to cross between a thousand thoughts. The first and most powerful thought was whether he had gone to her room while I was in a deep sleep. I wanted to ask but didn't want to cause unnecessary mistrust if it was not the case. But the thought kept coming again and again.

One day, I met Lal's three friends, Piyal, Sunil and Siva, in the office corridor on the ground floor. Usually everyone went out of the office for a short walk or to buy some lunch. These three long-time friends who worked in the same office always went together. Siva was a quiet person and but the other two were talkative. Piyal said, 'We heard Lal stayed with you for a night on his last visit.'

'Yes,' I answered.

'And you had lots of drinks …' Piyal continued.

'Yes.'

They laughed and went away. On another occasion, both Piyal and Sunil asked, 'Can we come to your place for a drink?'

'Why not?' I said.

Then both Piyal and Sunil said they also wanted to stay overnight and as they walked off, they were laughing loudly. I sensed something had gone wrong, but I didn't know what it was. Siva cut short from the other two and came back to me.

In short, he said, 'Please try to avoid those two because they are making fun of you.' I couldn't believe it as they were not my close friends. I hardly knew them other than saying 'hello' when we saw each other. I said to Siva, 'I don't get it – tell me why.'

'I cannot tell you all about it – you are just better to avoid them,' he said.

After I repeated my question about a thousand times more, he agreed to tell me what he'd heard, but made me promise not to behave any differently with my wife, to fight or even have an argument with her. I promised.

On the day Lal stayed with us, he could not sleep, as I was snoring loudly. In the middle of the night, he sat on the mattress wide awake thinking, what will I do now? Then he remembered Suramya was looking at him out of the corner of her eye while he was playing with Kumudu. He noticed this a few times. On one occasion, their eyes met, and she smiled. He thought about going upstairs to Suramya's room and giving it a go. As he entered the room, he saw she was sleeping with the two kids, and he touched her and kissed while she was still asleep. Since there was no response, he went further and had sex with her. In the middle of it, she awoke, and he said, 'What do we do if Senevi comes?' Her answer was that she would pretend she was fast asleep.

'This is what I heard,' said Siva. 'That is why those two were asking to sleep at your place after a drink. Please avoid them as much as possible.'

My head started swirling, and I felt short of breath; I was burning with anger. I went back to my office and sat on my chair. Was this the reason he telephoned home? And how he got the phone number? Was this the reason why she said don't sleep with your friends on the ground floor? Was this the reason before he departed she came out to say goodbye? And what did they talk about in that two minutes of chat and laughter? Was this the reason she did not tell me on the day he phoned? Or was this only a rumour that had been spread? It was the ultimate betrayal. I told Jay I had a headache and went home, still thinking of what had happened. Was Suramya attracted to Lal's look? He looked like her lover Wickrama, but littler, shorter and with no moustache.

Lost in thought, I forgot to get off the train at the Wentworthville station and ended up in Blacktown. I had to take another train back to Wentworthville. I went straight to the bottle shop and bought the usual bottle of wine and went home. Still with a heavy head, I stayed home that evening mostly with the children, but with very little talking to anyone. A thousand times I thought of asking Suramya, but I did not. Even if I asked, who would say 'yes' anyway? It might only lead to arguments and hurt three little children and nothing else. I decided not to talk about it and remained silent, but I was in extreme hurt and pain. **This was a silent pain.**

In the morning, I went to the office in fear, wondering whether I would meet those guys, or for that matter, any Sri Lankan guys. I did not know how many others knew about this and I took a step back socially. The impact not only affected my office work, but life at home as well. The writing of my thesis was further delayed amid the unrest. Almost every day after work, I would bring a bottle of wine home, otherwise I could not sleep as my mind crossed to various incidents that had happened.

My blood pressure started to rise and one night went up to 250 mg systolic pressure. We called an ambulance and went to Westmead Hospital. On another occasion, in the office I got a chest pain, with a squeezing pressure and tightness. I thought I was having a heart attack. I telephoned home and talked to the children, thinking this might be the last time. I was worried about how, if I died, the children would survive and who would look after them? Colleagues called a taxi, and I went straight to the doctor, and he directed me to a cardiologist in Westmead. After a check, the cardiologist wanted to monitor the heart for 24 hours and attached a heart monitor with a number of wires running across the chest. When I came home Tirath said that my chest looked like the back of a TV. The following day, the cardiologist ruled out a heart attack but said it could be mild angina.

Life had to go on, and I went to work as usual, but I stopped the usual midday going out to avoid possible meetings with Lal's friends. At home, the children noticed something was wrong with me. Almost every day, I had to monitor my blood sugar and blood pressure. This was fun for little Sirimath. He used to come and sit near me and say 'ah pressure' when the machine started. Kumudu noticed that I was not talking or playing with them much. When I was sitting on the couch sullen, she would come close and start tickling me, saying in Sinhalese '*kithi kithi gee.*' The innocent little mind could not understand anything, but she was merely trying to make me laugh and be happy. Some days, I did not want to share the bed with Suramya and took the mat downstairs and slept on it. Some days, little Kumudu said, 'I want to sleep with *Achchi*, I don't kick in the night like *Malli* (Sirimath),' and she came and slept with me. Perhaps she deeply felt my changes. I was determined to make my children's future bright, however; they were three innocent children, and their parents' faults should not cause them to suffer.

Despite everything I was going through, in a herculean effort, I completed the thesis. The first thing I did was stop drinking, so I could stay awake at night. Only on the weekend would I bring a bottle of wine home, though I was still smoking. After office hours, I would come home and, after dinner, start working on the thesis as well as writing technical papers for publication. I finally managed to submit the thesis to Flinders University for examination. By this time, most of the current projects at the office were nearing completion, and I thought, before starting any new work, I might find employment somewhere else, preferably in an international organisation. I started to submit applications to a few organisations and one day happened to see an advertisement stating that the Ministry of Water Resources in Oman was looking for water resource experts. I made an application after talking to my supervisor at the university who had worked in Oman for a number of years.

Within three months, I received a telephone call from Oman that I had been selected for the position. The person said he was from the sponsoring company as the Ministry did not hire external experts directly and asked me to fill in a number of forms and complete medical certificates. He briefly explained the facilities in Oman, as it was a modern country. With regards to the children's schooling, he said there was a Sri Lankan school there, and if we preferred, we could even send the children to British or American schools in Muscat. The tax-free salary package was very attractive.

In addition, the total package included a furnished family home, a four-wheel-drive vehicle, annual return airfares to Sydney and annual leave. It was a tremendous relief. We all talked about this, and everyone was very excited and happy to go to a new country. I joked to Tirath saying, 'In Oman, you have to go to school on a camel's back,' and we all laughed. Suramya said, 'Before we go, I want to go to Sri Lanka and see mother.' I arranged for them to go at the end of school and I followed them.

Everyone in Sri Lanka, both sides of the family, were very happy that I was going to be closer to them. We could save and even build a house in Sri Lanka. On the day I arrived, before dinner, I had a drink with Daya *Aiya*. Usually, we would go to the backyard behind the house for a drink. After a few drinks, I told him about the stresses I went through, the office work, completing my thesis and the rumour about his sister's infidelity. I told the full story from A-Z, what Suramya had said and what I heard from Lal's friends. He was surprised and said, '*Malli*, when I heard all this, it is believable, but he might have come to her room, and she might have chased him out. With that anger, he might well have spread a rumour. I don't think *Nangi* would do such a thing.' I said 'That might well be.' But what I didn't say was, 'Then why did he telephone our home?' I told Daya *Aiya* that I wanted to meet with a psychologist before going to Oman, which he organised. It was the same lady psychologist in the same private hospital. She recognised me as I entered her room. After hearing the full story, all she said was the problem would still continue, and as no one had seen whether it actually happened, I should try to ignore it. She prescribed anti-depression tablets for me to take to calm down. Most importantly she told me to think about the children's future and that I was living for them.

In early 1994, I received an external examination report on the thesis from the university. After the necessary corrections, it was submitted to the university, and I was accepted for the award of a PhD degree. What an effort for a family man with three young children and the worst endless marriage problems. After receiving the appointment letter, air tickets and other documents, I applied to the department for one year's leave without pay, which was granted as a special case to obtain my services later.

We decided to go to Oman, initially myself alone to settle and, later, the family would join me. Up until then, the family would stay in Suramya's mother's house in Udahagama. We all went to Sri Lanka, and I left for Oman in April 1994. By this time my drinking habit had almost completely stopped except with Suramya's brothers. While we were in Sri Lanka at Suramya's mother's house, Suramya told me that Podi *Aiya* (Wickrama)'s wife was very cruel to him and he was not happy. I asked how she knew and also why she was telling me this. Suramya's reply was surprising: she told me her mother had told her. Suramya could not see her own cruelty towards her husband, but was now sympathising over her lover's suffering.

A noticeable thing was that since Lal left our house on that infamous day, he never telephoned me, not even to say thank you for allowing me to stay in your home. Since then, he might have visited head office several times but had not come to see me as before. I never heard from him or saw him again.

The pain of infidelity is unlike any other. It consumes
a person, emotionally and physically. It calls forth
a roller coaster of primal feelings of rage, abandonment
and loss. And surviving the pain of infidelity takes a
herculean effort at a time when the betrayed spouse
has nothing left to give.

-Mary Ellen Goggin-

Chapter 7

Life in Oman

I arrived in Oman alone. There was a representative from the sponsoring company to receive me. He took me to a hotel in Ruwi and said my meals and accommodation would be paid for by the company, and tomorrow morning he would come and pick me up to take me to the Ministry of Water Resources.

The following day, at the Ministry I met the director general of Water Resources Management. He described the general organisation of the Ministry and the areas of responsibility of each department, as well as introducing me to several directors. I was assigned to the Water Resources Protection Department, with multiple responsibility areas in protecting wellfields and water supply aquifers. There were several areas of new knowledge required, such as isotope hydrology and hydrochemistry. I started self-learning, going through several textbooks and the PhD thesis of my supervisor, *Hydrogeology of Oman Mountains*, which was considered one of the leading publications at the time. The working hours in the Ministry were from 7:30 am to 2:30 pm, so I had enough time to study.

The following day, the company official came to pick me to take to their company and introduce me to the staff. He took me around the Muscat and Ruwi area and showed me the location of the Sri Lankan school and various shopping centres. Within two weeks, I was given a Toyota Landcruiser. After a month, I was given some furnished family accommodation in Wadi Kabir, close to the Sri Lankan school. I settled in the house and took some photos of the Landcruiser and the home and posted them to Sri Lanka for the family to see how Oman looked. The children were very excited.

Two weeks after I moved into the house, the family joined me. I showed them around Ruwi and Muscat and we familiarised ourselves with the country. Tirath and Kumudu were admitted to the school, and we arranged for school transport with a trustworthy driver, Chandran, who picked them up in the morning and dropped them off in the afternoon. Sirimath started school a little later. Initially, he cried about going to school, and one day I had to make the painful decision to take a little stick from the front yard Magosa tree to hit rump. Sirimath cried, but thereafter he never made a fuss about going to school.

The children liked the school. Sirimath had a dedicated teacher, Mrs Nesiah, who even took time teaching children at her home. Kumudu had a favourite class teacher, who she called 'Shriyani teacher.' Sometimes Kumudu imitated the teacher at home, teaching her pretend students very seriously. She even applied some red lipstick, just like the teacher. Tirath had a number of good teachers, all very dedicated. All three of the children built their networks of friends, and some of their parents were my friends as well. Suramya also made some friends, as we would attend social events organised by the Sri Lankan community such as the new year festival, fundraising events, religious events at the embassy premises, Daham Pasala (a school for teaching Buddhism to children) and Pirith (reciting Buddhist sutras) ceremonies at residential houses. The Pirith reciting was not really a religious event, rather it was more of an opportunity to meet people. Each family brought a dish to share and after the Pirith, we all enjoyed the food. Suramya's Pol Sambola (coconut sambal) was one of the favourites. Thus, our networking and social life with other community members drastically improved.

As taxes were low for almost all imported goods in Oman, grocery items and clothes were cheaper than either Sri Lanka or in Australia. There were numerous restaurants in Ruwi: Indian, Pakistani, Lebanese and other Middle Eastern places. For the first time, we ate Indian foods such as chapati, paratha, paneer palak, a variety of chicken and mutton masalas. At least once a week, we went to the nearby restaurant, usually on Thursday night, for a special meal. In addition, we would go out and buy a dish or whatever the children liked to eat such as KFC, pizza, burger and even roast chicken. There was a variety of freshly caught fish available in Mathra fish market. I would go there and buy fish for a week or two, clean them and store them in the freezer. Once Suramya and the children came, and on seeing the large tuna fish, Kumudu screamed as she was scared of them. Thereafter, she never came again. Sirimath was the one who always liked to come with me to a shop or the fish market. It was nice having him around, as he kept talking. Usually, he wanted a snack and a bottle of drink. One day, when we were driving home from the fish market, he asked for a drink bottle, finished half and said, 'The other half is for *Akka*.' A few minutes later, he started to suck more from the straw and then said, 'The remainder is for *Akka*.' This went on until we reached home, and by this time, the bottle was empty. At least he was concerned for his sister. I used to call Tirath '*Lokuputha*' (eldest son). For Kumudu, we had a variety of names such as '*Chuti Amma*' (little mother), '*Chuti Duwa*' (little daughter), '*Mage Duwa*' (my daughter) or '*Mage Amma*' (my mother). Sirimath was always '*Thutta*' (little one), or '*Chuti Putha*' (little son), '*Malli*' or just '*Chutta*' (little one).

There were many jewellery shops in Ruwi. Most of the designs were to attract the expatriate community: Sri Lankan, Indian, Pakistani and Bangladeshi. It was a traditional custom to provide your own wife and daughters as well as to give gifts to close relatives. We started to collect jewellery for Suramya and Kumudu, and then to expand to nieces on both sides of the family. After several years, we collected so much jewellery for Kumudu – no other girl on either side of the family had ever had that much through the generations. One day, a thought came across my mind that though we only have one daughter now, in the future there will be two other daughters who will join the family when Tirath and Sirimath got married, so we started to collect jewellery for our future daughters-in-law. Tirath joked that he would sell this jewellery and make his wife earrings from a can of coke, which annoyed his mother.

Before coming to Oman, I had a plan to create savings, which I discussed with Suramya. At least half my salary would be saved in Australia to buy a house; a quarter of my salary would be saved in Sri Lanka in a dollar account so we could build a house there; and the rest of my salary would be for our living and travel expenses and to help my family in Sri Lanka. Once I noticed that the monthly telephone bill was exceeding 300 rials, which was equivalent to the monthly salary of a technical officer or junior engineer. I explained the reason we were there was to save money and not to pay telephone bills. As usual, Suramya blamed it on my sister, Sudu *Akka*, saying it was she who asked her to telephone. But I knew, in reality, it was hours of talking with Chitra *Akka*, her popular sister. I explained to her that working there was not easy, as there were two groups of people among the workforce earning different amounts, which made things difficult. One group was Sri Lankan, Indian, Asian and African, and my salary was much higher than theirs. This was because, in Oman, salary was based on where the employee was hired from. The other group was from western countries, and since

I had been working in Australia, I was on the higher salary scale. This was not an easy environment to survive because I was of Asian origin and people were jealous. There was always someone there to find fault, therefore I had to work harder than anyone, doing two- or three-times the work the average expert would do.

While I was at work, Suramya was at home. So she could keep up her reading habit, we became members of a second handbook shop in Qurum Commercial Centre, where you could buy a book and resell it to the shop for half price. In this way, you could read any amount of books at a low cost. In addition to exchange, one could sell one's old books to the shop.

Towards the end of the year, we started to buy gifts to take to Sri Lanka, for all the family members on both sides; mainly clothes and dresses for the children, sarees for the ladies and shirts for the grown-up males. At the end of the year, the children got a long school vacation, so we had enough time to spend with our families. I also applied for annual leave. One day, our Sri Lankan neighbour, Srinath, asked whether I had sent cargo boxes to Sri Lanka. I said we are taking the gifts in suitcases. Then he explained. In the Middle East, at least two months before the travel date, you could ship your cargo through a Sri Lankan company – anything you liked. It was very cheap and you could send relatively large quantities, even food items. Thereafter, that's what we did too rather than carrying it in suitcases. In addition to clothes, canned food was expensive in Sri Lanka, such as corned beef, canned cheese, sausages, biscuits, pasta and sauces, canned and dried fruits, even coffee and olives.

At the end of the year, during the long school holiday period, we went to Sri Lanka, the third visit in a year. Everyone was happy to see us, and the children were delighted to see their cousins, aunts and uncles. We divided the time between my sister in Kurunegala and Suramya's house. When we were in Kurunegala, we organised day-trips by hiring a bus to go to many historical places such as Kalawewa, Sigiriya, Polonnaruwa, Mihintale and Anuradhapura with close relatives. By this time, I had restarted my photography hobby and took lots of family photos. Later on, when the children were older, only our family made visits to interesting and scenic places in Sri Lanka, such as Nuwara Eliya, World's End in Horton Place, and stopped over at a number of beautiful waterfalls and areas where I worked on the Mahaweli project and also to see the *Veddah* people in Dambana. Kumudu was scared to see them and have her photo taken with them.

In Oman, we visited all the major historical places such as the forts in Nakhal, Bahla, Mutrah and Nizwa. There were beautiful beaches we visited as a family, sometimes with family friends. In addition to beaches close to Muscat, we also visited places further away, such as Sohar Beach. Visits to Oman's interior were amazing. We all enjoyed trips to the oases, with their dates palms and other crops and trees, particularly lime and mangos. I explained to the children how the ancient water channels known as 'aflaj' were dug and maintained to irrigate the land using a sundial, at least historically. The UNESCO World Heritage Falaj Daris in Nizwa was one of the remarkable, and after the visit, we would go for lunch at a nearby restaurant. Several other times, we had a picnic with friends. One of these memorable trips was with Somachandra's family. We took lunch and water with us so we could stay a full day at the Wadi bed. At one point, we decided to climb a nearby rock. The mothers and the two girls stayed at the Wadi bed while we climbed the rock. I let Sirimath go first, and I followed him in case he slipped so I could catch him. Sirimath, like an experience rock climber, gave me instructions while he was climbing, like '*Achchi*, keep your foot here, hold this piece of rock,' and sometimes he looked down asking, 'Are you OK *Achchi*?' What a little son, so concerned about his father. When we were about to reach the top, Sirimath said, 'Oh, my pants are falling down, but life is more important than pants,' because he had to hold on to the rock; he knew that if he didn't, he would fall. When we came down, we told this story to the others, and all laughed about the cheeky Sirimath.

At the Ministry office, I learned that my contract was going to be renewed for another year. But this time, instead of a sponsoring company, the Ministry would hire me directly. This was good news. In 1995, Suramya said she wanted to go to Sri Lanka to see her mother during the school holidays in the middle of the school year, to which I agreed. The working days in Oman were Saturday to Wednesday; Thursdays and Fridays are the weekends. One week after Suramya and the children went to Sri Lanka, I had to stay at home to rest a twisted ankle. The following Monday afternoon, I received a telephone call and answered 'hello,' not knowing who it was. Normally I telephoned Sri Lanka to talk to family rather than they telephone me. To my surprise, from the other end of the line I heard, 'Uhh, it is Lal here, just inquiring about how you are doing in Oman?'

I was so shocked, I couldn't talk and hung up the phone. I felt a headache beginning, and a pain in my chest and I sat down. It took several hours to recover. I had no doubt then that the rumour spread in the Sydney office was true; it was quite clear to me. And for the first time, I decided to tell Suramya not to come back. I wrote a letter describing all the painful incidents she had caused and asked her not to come back. I also told her I was going to cancel her visa. I asked her to hand over the children to me. This was the harshest possible letter I had ever written, possibly that *any* husband had written to his wife. With some difficulty, I went to Ruwi and posted the letter. The same weekend, some friends, Wasantha and Mayuri, came to see me with their daughter. I told them I wasn't well and had a little chest pain, so I was resting at home. They said it may be because the family had gone to Sri Lanka and I was living alone. They told me they were planning to go to Nizwa and invited me to join them rather than staying at home alone, to which I agreed.

By this time, my anger had gone, and I was thinking of the children's education and future. I realised I had taken a very harsh stance that would destroy my own children's future. On my return to Muscat, I telephoned Suramya at her mother's house and told her she would get a letter and not to open it and to bring it back when she returned. But by this time, she had already read the letter and told Daya *Aiya* about it. She said that somehow, she would look after the children, and she had talked with my sister Kumari and together they would look after the children. At this point, I felt sorry for her and my sister.

The following day, Daya *Aiya* telephoned from his office and asked me what had happened. I briefed him, as he was aware of the previous incident as well. He told me he brought Suramya and the children to his home in Colombo and was now looking for a school for the children. It struck me hard what the psychologist told me: 'You have to forget everything for the sake of the children.' If I didn't bring them back, the education of three brilliant children would be jeopardised. I told him there was no need to send the children to school in Sri Lanka and to send them back to Oman at the end of their holiday. I told him I had not cancelled Suramya's visa. Then Daya *Aiya* replied that Suramya was worried I would mistreat her, to which I reassured him I would never do it. The same day, late in the evening, Sudu *Akka* telephoned and asked me to come to Sri Lanka to see the psychologist again, as I may be undergoing the depression. She also said I should come to Colombo to discuss it – but she didn't know about the rumour. However, at the end of the holiday period, the family came back to Oman to resume the children's schooling. The day they arrived, Daya *Aiya* telephoned to verify how Suramya and the children were doing. Suramya later told me she had told Tirath about the incident and at first he had refused to come back to Oman.

Everything returned to normal when they arrived home, as I had badly needed them. We didn't talk about the telephone call or any incident that had happened in the past. Meantime, my contract was transferred to the Ministry, and I was initially given a furnished rental home in Madinat Qaboos, and later, a large house in the same area owned by the Ministry, which had previously been a guest house. We gave the large upstairs room to Tirath. My community activity expanded as I was contributing voluntary service as a board member of the management of the Sri Lankan school. By this time, a new school had been built with many facilities and a well-equipped laboratory and classrooms.

As the children were growing up, they started after-school activities and after work, I would go to pick them up. Tirath was maturing fast, proving his nickname at the Westmead school of 'the walking encyclopedia.' He won every spelling contest organised by the Indian Social Club and scrabble contests organised by the Sri Lankan Community Social Club. We were also passing through very interesting childhood periods for Kumudu and Sirimath. One day after school, I picked Kumudu up from the school and was driving home. On the way she said, 'I want chips,' to which I answered, 'There are no shops open at this time of day, my daughter.' She was not happy; she looked out the window and wouldn't talk to me until we reached home. On another occasion, one weekend, I was working at the computer which was kept in Kumudu's room. Sirimath came in and sat on one side of the bed. I didn't ask why. A little while later, Kumudu came and sat on the other side of the bed, and still no one was talking. I knew something had gone wrong between them. They often fought and then became friends in the next minute, so Suramya and I decided not to get involved. Sirimath broke the silence: '*Achchi,* in my next life I want to become an elder son not the youngest.'

Then Kumudu started to cry, saying 'That is because he wants to hit me, but he cannot do that because I am the *Akka* [elder sister].'

This was the kind of childhood they had. At least Sirimath had the manners not to hit his *Akka.* And Kumudu cried for the pain that would be incurred in the next life – very pleasant memories that will last until my final breath.

To give the children overall development, we decided to enrol them in karate classes conducted by an Omani instructor. Classes were on weekends, so there were no disturbances to their homework. In addition, we took them swimming in the Hyatt Regency hotel swimming pool. Several times I went to the pool with them and asked Kumudu and Sirimath to swim in the shallow end of the pool. When they got used to the pool, I asked the instructor to keep an eye on them while Suramya and I did our workout in the gym. In the evening at home, usually after dinner, we watched cricket matches during the season or films and Indian musical shows on the Indian television networks such as Zee TV. In addition, we watched the BBC news. All channels were freely available.

One day, Suramya said that she received a letter from Priyani, who had written about building a house in Sri Lanka. She started nagging that all her friends had houses, only she didn't have one. I explained again and again the reason we were saving money in Sri Lanka was so that one day we could build a house on the land.

'Further,' I said, 'right now we don't need a house as the first and foremost thing is to buy a house in Sydney and educate the children.'

But she didn't listen, and continued nagging day after day, adding trouble to our lives, which had at that point been relatively happy. Finally, I agreed. I met an Indian architect and drew a plan for a large two-storey house. Then I told her brother Nandimitra to find a contractor to prepare the land, particularly to build a retaining wall along the roadside and prepare an access road for the building site. In addition, we registered the plan with the local council and obtained municipal water supply to the land. All ancillary works done except building the house.

We had visited most of the historical places in Sri Lanka as the children were growing up, so I decided to visit overseas countries during the long school holidays. On our trips, we stopped over in Sri Lanka to see our families. In addition, Suramya and the children visited Sri Lanka in the mid-term holidays. One of the setbacks that occurred by going away during the end-of-year school holidays was that Kumudu couldn't have her birthday party with her friends as we were always somewhere else. But there was no way around it, so we did a little celebration as much as we could. During this time, we visited India, Australia, Thailand and the UAE.

India was interesting. The trip was organised by one of my colleagues, Ramakumar, who came from Delhi. He arranged a van with a driver for us to travel through India, from Delhi to Bodh Gaya through Varanasi and back to Delhi via Agra, to see the Taj Mahal. As we had been warned as foreigners not to eat food from roadside shops, I was very careful not to consume any such food. We sometimes had to travel quite far between meals that were at least at a three-star hotel or restaurant. Sometimes everyone was hungry, but only talkative Sirimath was the one to make a fuss, frequently asking how many kilometres we had to go, every five or ten minutes. I felt sorry for him, but keeping them away from gastric problems was more important. At Bodh Gaya, we crossed the Neranjana River and went to see the place where the beautiful farmer's wife, Sujata, offered rice milk to the Buddha. By this time, the children had studied some of these Buddhist teachings from their Dhamma school.

In Thailand, we hired a van organised by another friend Jayasooriya, and travelled through some interesting places in Bangkok such as the crocodile park, elephant park, Golden Buddha statue, Wat Pho temple, floating market in Chao Phraya River and the Grand Palace. We also went to see the River Kwai and passed through many beautiful towns like Nakhon Pathom. At the River Kwai, we went to the JEATH War Museum, about the Death Railway built by prisoners of war during the Second World War.

In 1997, we travelled to Australia and spent the first few days staying with Gamini and Lali. The children enjoyed catching up with their friends after three years away. Before I went to Sydney, I wrote to Gamini and told him I was interested in getting a home loan and buying a house close to where they lived. By this time, they had bought a house in Carlingford. Gamini very kindly took us to several houses, and there was also a vacant block very close to them for sale. In the end, I didn't buy the land or a house though, as there was talk going around that, after the Olympic Games, house prices would drop and it would be better to wait until then. But what happened was house prices skyrocketed. This was another silly mistake, among others.

In 1997, another incident happened. One day when I returned home from the Ministry, I saw Suramya with a sad face and red eyes. I asked her what had happened. She told me Podi *Aiya* (Wickrama) had died and that the woman he had married had not looked after him. He died from pneumonia. She telephoned several houses to inquire about it, including my sister Kumari. I patiently watched my wife grieving over the death of her lover. What else could I do? Several days later, Suramya told me she was worried Chitra would take revenge on her for not marrying her brother. But worse than that, in time, Suramya's fear changed to anger and she began to suspect everything that Chitra *Akka* did was about taking revenge.

My contract with the Ministry continued. The children were doing well in their studies and co-curricular activities. Finally, Tirath reached year 11 and sat for the GCE London examination. He did well, getting straight As for all subjects. Next, it was time for his advanced level classes, and I thought of settling the family in Sydney and sending him to a high school there. I knew I could return to my previous workplace there. However, Suramya insisted she wanted to go to Adelaide, as Daya *Aiya* and Chitra *Akka* were there for her if any help was needed. I agreed, and in June 2000 we moved to Adelaide, though I planned to return to work in Oman for the time being.

We initially staying at Daya *Aiya*'s house for two weeks until we bought a house in Magill. We enrolled Tirath at the Norwood-Morialta High School and Kumudu and Sirimath at Magill Primary School. The house was close to both schools, so the children could walk there. With the rest of our savings, I bought a second-hand car and Suramya obtained her drivers' licence though she had to go through the learning process again. She could then go shopping, visit Daya *Aiya*'s place and pick up the children from the school if needed. Before I left, we organised an evening tea party for the neighbours to introduce ourselves and the family. It was a lovely neighbourhood.

After three months, I heard lots of complaining about Daya *Aiya* and Chitra *Akka* from Suramya. Daya *Aiya* was asking her often for money, and Chitra *Akka* ignored her in the presence of her friend.

She had even told Suramya that from now on Suramya had to listen to her, as she had been the first one to come to Adelaide. This was a personality clash. In addition, Suramya carried the hidden fear that Chitra would take revenge on her.

Over time, Suramya underwent a hysterectomy and two knee operations. She cooked and kept food in the fridge before she was admitted to hospital and asked us not to eat anything from her brother's house or anything that Chitra *Akka* might bring us while she was in the hospital. Her fear was that Chitra might poison her family. As promised, we never had anything from them.

I came home twice a year, and the family came to Oman once a year. One day, Daya *Aiya* asked us to come to his place. Usually, we would go together as a family, but when we got there, they were sitting at the dining table with another couple. Their children, Nandana and Nandani were apparently in their rooms, maybe attending to their own school work. Daya *Aiya* introduced the couple; the husband, Susantha, was a lawyer and his wife, who hailed from Allawwa area, was in fact a relative of my Punchi *Akka*'s husband, Nilame *Aiya*. After a short discussion, Daya *Aiya* spoke to us in front of our children about getting social security benefits for us if we separated temporarily and then reunited again when I returned from Oman permanently. He said the lawyer could help us with the separation and, again, the reuniting. I couldn't believe it. This man was telling his sister to separate from her husband to defraud the government and fraudulently claim social security benefits. Both the lawyer and Dayananda told us there were many people doing this. I was silent up to that point and then told them both I wouldn't do anything against the law and my heart. If I had no money, I would beg on the street. It was quite clear that their intention was to obtain social security money for them. We had absolutely no need of it.

After we got home, I told Suramya I had no respect for her brother whatsoever, telling his sister to separate from her husband to rob the government of money – such a scoundrel of a person. Suramya tried to clean her brother's name by saying, 'That woman, Chitra, might have asked him to do it, otherwise he would not.'

Whatever happened, we continued to visit them, but with caution. I mostly stayed outside the house playing darts in the backyard. On one of my holidays, Suramya told me that Chitra continue to harass her in front of others. On one occasion when she telephoned, she was rude and said she was busy making short eats. This incident had caused Suramya deep pain. One day, she answered the phone and started shouting at Chitra, telling her all that she had done; it was almost like in Sri Lanka when she was fighting with her mother. Abusive words went on despite me telling her to stop it. As the language became worse, I took Kumudu and Sirimath to their rooms and went to the lounge area. The abusive language continued and again I signalled for her to stop, but she didn't. So I went out the back door with Tirath. I did not want him to hear those filthy words. We went inside the house after the phone call ended. Suramya said she had wanted to express that for a long time.

A little later, we saw Dayananda's car parked on the road; he was coming to our house. Suramya said that he must be planning to apologise to her, after blaming Chitra. She was confident about her brother. But what happened was quite the opposite. He sat on the couch and started to blame her for accusing his wife. At one point he said, 'You have told her even that you looked after our children in the past.' Dayananda was blaming his sister in front of our children. I didn't say anything except, 'Was it right not to introduce your sister and her children to your visitors at home? How would you feel if I didn't introduce you to my friends when you were visiting our home?' He agreed it was wrong, but explained that Chitra had thought there was no reason to introduce her, as they were all relatives. He said let's just continue the relationship as it was. But I thought otherwise. It was a recipe for more troubles. I'd had enough, and that was the last time we met, since we didn't have anything in common.

The children were growing fast. Tirath had become one of the finest young men I had ever seen. His honesty and the way he took responsibility and helped others were among the finest qualities he had. Academically, he was still the best. Suramya once said to me he even took a father's role, at times guiding his younger sibling. He helped his mother keep the home and garden tidy. It was a big relief for me. We still talked on the internet, almost every day. I never wanted to miss that. Kumudu and Sirimath were still cuddly and they would tell me their daily activities, starting from 'waking up early morning.' Once Kumudu had a little cut on her finger, and almost every day she showed me with a tender voice. By 2001, the Ministry underwent reorganization and as a result, higher salary expatriate staff had to be reduced. I was one of them and we were informed about it. Some former colleagues were working at Petroleum Development Oman, and they contacted me and said there was an opportunity for a groundwater modeller coming in the near future. I expressed my interest, as I was still not financially secure enough to guarantee a comfortable life for the family. I needed to work until the children finished their tertiary education. I told Suramya about the opportunity, but at the end of the Ministry contract I would come home to see them. The following day, Suramya told me that last night she and Tirath had heard Kumudu crying in her room. When asked why, she told them she'd heard *Achchi* was not going to come home. This brought tears to my eyes, and I told Suramya that everything I was doing was for them – to give my children the comfort I did not have. I was alone there and not happy about it. So at the end of the contract, I came home.

My purpose of continuing to live with Suramya had produced results. Tirath got excellent results in his high-school examinations. Our family lives were so interesting – I couldn't imagine living without them. I was there for them. I am there for them.

Family I love
In the valley of love
Love of family is so strong,
It's not for some time,
It's for throughout and so long,
I oh so love my family so much,
I will forever stay with them,
Coz they are my true support.

-Wish A Friend-

Chapter 8

No moneyman

In 2001 I came home. There were no jobs available in Adelaide; I was looking for an interstate position or even an opportunity overseas. My final payment and provident fund from the Ministry in Oman were sufficient to pay off the home loan. However, our savings were rapidly diminishing. I had three growing teenagers, and I wanted to pay their university fees to send them into the world so they could start living their lives loan-free. My contact in Oman informed me that the position in the oil company had still not been formalised.

It was around 10 am, and I was reading the *Sunday Observer* newspaper at the dining table when the phone rang. Suramya usually answered the phone. As a matter of fact, I was not in the habit of making phone calls. But Suramya was in the kitchen at the sink washing something, so I answered the phone and said 'Hello.' The reply was strange – a male voice – it was Lal, who said he was in Adelaide with his daughter for a medical faculty interview and wanted to see me. He asked for directions to our place. I couldn't speak for a minute, then I said, 'I don't want to see you ever again. You spread some bad things about me when we were in Sydney,' and I put the phone down. My head was heavy and swirling and I felt the same pain in my chest as before, which was a sign of increased blood pressure. When I went to go into the lounge room to sit down, Suramya asked me who it was.

'Lal,' I said, and she asked how he knew the number. 'I don't know,' was my response, though my feeling was that she had given it to him. I had more questions without answers, like how he knew I had settled in Adelaide; how he knew I was home from Oman. Nobody knew, except the family. It was clear to me Suramya somehow knew he would telephone, and just to hear my response, had pretended to be washing something. It was not cooking or washing time. Over the last seven years, he had never talked to me except accidentally when I picked up the phone in Oman in 1995. After leaving our house, he had never come to see me in the office or even telephoned me when we were in Sydney. I sat in the lounge for the next few hours until my headache went away. I would never talk about it again. There was no need as I would never find a solution and there were three beautiful teenagers at home. The words of the psychologist were deeply embedded within me: 'You have to live for them.'

I was receiving emails from Oman informing me the hydrogeologist modeller position for the oil company had been further delayed. As there was no job in Adelaide, I went to the social security office and registered as an unemployed. To get the benefit, I had to periodically visit the office with details of jobs that I had applied for over the last two weeks. One day, I got a telephone call in response to one of the positions I had applied for, from a Gold Coast consultancy company. The person was in fact visiting Adelaide and was happy to have an informal interview, which later proved successful. The position was for a hydrologist modeller, basically modelling surface and river flows.

My friend Randeva found a rental place for me about one kilometre from the office. It was a part of a garage, converted to a rental unit. Randeva kindly showed me around the town and office, and occasionally came on weekends to take me to their house for dinner. The help I received from Randeva was more than one would expect from a friend. The work was stressful as I had to meet a number of deadlines in a short space of time. One day I had to stay in the office overnight to complete urgent works. The family had tried to contact me, but I was nowhere to be found, and they had telephoned friends to ask them to try to locate me. The following day, I telephoned home and told them I might leave this company. By this time, some good news had come from Oman about the groundwater modeller's position, which was about to be filled. I discussed it with Tirath and Suramya and they were happy. I talked to the consultancy company manager and left the job, and within three months, I was jobless again.

After another two months, I received a telephone call from the oil company – I had been selected for the position of senior hydrogeologist–groundwater modelling. The salary level was western direct hire, which meant an attractive salary plus other benefits, including family accommodation in the camp, children's school fees, business class travel from Oman to Australia and free medical treatment from the company clinic. Everyone was very happy as this was a once-in-a-lifetime position. By this time, our savings had declined further, and we even found it difficult to pay the orthodontist to fix Sirimath's teeth.

After receiving my visa, about two weeks before I was due to go, Suramya started making a fuss that I was going back to Oman. I explained again and again that I couldn't find a job in Adelaide or even Australia, and here I had secured one of the finest jobs in the world. I explained our responsibilities towards the children in terms of educating them and paying their university fees so they wouldn't be left with a debt on graduating, and I also said that my life was not going to be easy there as I had to look after the house, cook for myself and have very little time left for anything else as working hours were from 7 am to 6 pm. I was not going on holiday, but to work hard for the benefit of our family.

As usual, she never listened; instead, she started to cry for no reason. I knew this was just her way of making trouble. She said somehow we could learn to live just off social security benefits. I repeatedly asked her to show me how to we could live like that, and every time her answer was, 'I will do it.' I knew she would start nagging, as we still had a bit of savings left. But she didn't say she would manage our expenditure carefully. She didn't say she would find a job; she just asked me to stay at home. She knew that I would quickly become angry and this way she could attract the children's attention to her. A mother's tears are very powerful, and Suramya had the ability to instantly cry and sometimes, in the next minute, laugh again.

When it became intolerable, I started to shout at her and reached to close her mouth by squeezing it. Tirath came towards me to hit me, and Sirimath and Kumudu also started to cry. A little later, Tirath also began crying and said, '*Amma* and *Achchi* are not loving each other, and I thought both of you did love each other.' This was what Suramya wanted; she wanted to get the attention of the children as sympathy for her. When I was shouting at Suramya, little Kumudu shouted at me saying, 'Don't hit *Amma!*' Still burning with anger, I shouted at her and said, 'Are you also trying to control me?' How good would it have been if Tirath, being a university student, could tell his mother that *Achchi* was going to work to give us comfortable lives instead of trying to hit me? How good would it have been if Suramya could say to me, 'It is alright for you to go and work in Oman; it is all for the sake of the family' and wished me well. But that was not her thing. So far in life, there had been no support – just trouble.

Because of the unbearable pain, I went to the liquor shop and bought a bottle of vodka and started to drink in the unused back rooms. I came to the main house only to drink water and use the toilet. My thoughts were that it was better to die than live like this. Later, I talked to Kumudu and Sirimath about why I was going back to Oman, and they seemed to fully understand.

It was not all bad going when I went back to Oman again. Tirath was a big help at home. Four times a week, we talked through video-conferencing on the internet – on a Thursday and Friday, which were the weekend in Oman, and Saturday and Sunday in Australia. This way we all could stay updated about what was happening in our lives, particularly from the children about their school activities. I felt sometimes they missed me, but thinking about my efforts in making their future bright left me with no regrets.

I was not involved in any community activity during this period, and talking to my lovely family was a big thing in breaking the loneliness. Each year, we again met three times: I went to Australia twice, and for the end-of-the-year long holiday, the family visited Oman. The first trip was exciting, as they could now travel in business class. They enjoyed their time in Oman. We went to see the school, the new shopping centres opened at Al Qurum and Seeb, and a number of times we went to the oil company's private beach. Everyone also enjoyed numerous meals out at restaurants. One day, Suramya apologised for the unnecessary fuss she had made before I left. Our savings were again building up, and I asked Suramya to prioritise, first and foremost, the fee for the orthodontist and the children's university fees.

One Saturday, when I was waiting for the children to come to the home computer, I found an interesting job advertisement for a hydrogeologist in Adelaide at the water utility company. As the closing date was within the next two days, I talked to the children and prepared my application and sent it through registered post. In response, I received a letter asking when I would be able to attend the interview, and within three months, I got the job. I left the oil company in December 2004, a day before the tsunami in the Indian Ocean. The family had come to Oman for their end-of-year school holidays, except for Tirath who was at home in Magill. On our way back to Australia, we made a visit to our families in Sri Lanka. Tirath telephoned and told us that my teacher friend Prof. John Argue had come to our home to find out how my family in Sri Lanka were. What a beautiful and kind person he was.

Since I was due to start my new job on 31 January 2005, I had almost a month of holiday after we got home, so we had trips to Kangaroo Island, Barossa Valley and Gorge gap wildlife park. Then it was time to start the new job. It was not difficult to adjust to the work, as I had done similar jobs in New South Wales and in Oman. But with this opportunity to live at home again, I would be able to see my children grow into some of the finest youths. Tirath was at the University of Adelaide studying dentistry and the other two were still in primary and middle schools. It was very interesting to talk with Tirath as he has become an independent thinker, typical in university life. He used to discuss issues such as whether we really need religion, and whether we should worry about some animal species declining as new species were always developing. Some of these talks were philosophical, just like discussions I had with his former principal, Somabandu Kodikara. It was really a pleasant father-son relationship. He continued to maintain his academic excellence at university as well, coming top of his class every year. He graduated in 2006. Later, Kumudu and

Sirimath also went to the University of Adelaide and excelled in their chosen fields, graduating with excellent results and finding employment in Adelaide.

In 2007 we sold our house in Magill and bought a relatively new house in Wattle Park. The house was on an elevated block with a magnificent view of the city and beyond. I thought, because of the view, one day we might be able to sell the house for a much higher price. Everyone, particularly Sirimath, said this house would be very difficult to sell because it was on the slope and in the end, that was what happened. Despite other family members' views, I bought the house. That was typical of me, either my way or the highway. I wasn't in the habit of consulting other family members and seeking a consensus. In 2007, I managed to cease smoking, a habit that had started in Sri Lanka around 1980.

By this time Tirath was working in Warrnambool, in Victoria. We visited several times and saw some interesting places. In 2008, Punchi *Akka* passed away. I did not attend the funeral. I have no regrets as I looked after my lovely sister very well while she was alive. In 2008, Nandimitra came to Adelaide for a holiday, and we took him to Warrnambool as well. One day, after his arrival, Nandimitra telephoned Dayananda and asked him to meet somewhere outside his house. To which apparently Dayananda replied, 'If you want to see me, you have to come to my place.' Nandimitra replied that he could not, because of Chitra and Nandani. The two brothers did not meet.

Around 2009, Suramya, Kumudu and I visited Sri Lanka. We stayed a few days in Kurunegala and went to Kandy to stay with Nandimitra. We visited Wasgamuwa National Park with Nandimitra. In 2010, Sudu *Akka* left the Kurunegala house to stay with Kumari *Nangi*, and the house has been kept closed since then.

At Nandimitra's house, an unbelievable incident happened. One day we were having breakfast, and after Nandimitra left, Nelum, Suramya, Kumudu, Sugandhika and I were sitting around the table. Sugandhika's second child, a daughter, had been born less than a month ago. Sugandhika had fallen in love with her batchmate, a handsome young man, now a surgeon in Kurunegala hospital. Nelum started to talk about her marriage and said that 'there were much better boys there for Sugandhika; why would she want to marry this man?' Everyone was surprised; Sugandhika rose from her chair angrily and left the room. I don't think anyone could believe this kind of comment after her own daughter had just had a second child. After all, had Nelum herself chosen the right person? She married her own first cousin, her mother's younger sister's son, which was a taboo in Sri Lanka. I couldn't stay there any longer and went out of the house to the veranda and sat there. My only thought was how many things this woman had said about my poor family. Suramya came out a little later and said, 'Sugandhika was very angry about what Nelum said.' I didn't talk about it much, but after we returned to Adelaide, I told Suramya not to ask me to go to Nandimitra's house again, as I didn't enjoy seeing that woman, Nelum. But in the end, since Suramya wasn't happy about this, I agreed we would continue to go there for the time that her brother was alive.

By this time, Tirath with in a relationship with a girl, Moly, from his senior year. She was working in Westmead Hospital, Sydney. When they visited Adelaide, Tirath brought her to our house to introduce her to the family. We were very happy about her, as she always had a pleasant smile and was soft spoken. After several visits, Tirath and Moly became engaged; he gave her the ring during one of her visits to our home when they went out for an evening walk. Suramya gave her the jewellery we bought when we were in Oman. This was one of the happiest days for me, as I had bought jewellery for my future daughter, and she had accepted them. Moly's parents invited us to their house for a dinner, which we gladly accepted. On that night, Moly was wearing the jewellery we gave her, and I was thrilled to see that.

Sirimath graduated in 2011 and was working in Adelaide. Tirath and Moly's marriage took place that same year in Adelaide. We were all very happy; it was a simple yet beautiful wedding ceremony. The entire cost was born by the couple from their savings. I was bit sad as I could not support my own son's wedding, whereas I was the one who paid for my sisters' and brother's weddings, and helped a niece with her wedding, but I didn't have any savings to give my son. By this time, I was a no-money man. All the expenditure was controlled by Suramya. She gave me a hundred dollars a week and another fifty dollars every two weeks for my bus ticket.

Tirath and Moly now have two lovely daughters: Lily, born in 2014 and Carla, born in 2015.

Eventually Kumudu graduated, as had Sirimath, from the University of Adelaide and started their working lives. In 2012, Suramya has received a message from Nandana that his father Dayananda was in a critical condition in the hospital and, if we wanted to, we were invited to come and see him.

They had mostly welcomed us. I was at the office, so I asked Suramya to go with the children, and told them I would join them at the hospital. Tirath was unable to join us, as he and Moly were working in Brisbane at the time. Eventually, Dayananda passed away, and the funeral took place at Centennial Park Cemetery. Nandimitra came to attend the funeral and stayed with us. I was happy to see Suramya was friendly with Chitra *Akka*; they were crying, holding each other's hands and sometimes embracing each other. After coming home, Suramya said she wanted to go to seventh-day alms giving and *Buddha puja* ceremony (giving alms to a Buddhist monk and listening to a sermon), which was taking place at Dayananda's house. Nandimitra said there was no need for that as we had already attended the funeral and that was enough. Suramya insisted, and we all participated in the *Buddha puja*. Suramya and the children went inside the house, but I stayed outside with other people. During the preaching, the monk from the Sri Lankan temple said that those who did not come to the temple were sinners and would burn in hell. The monk should not have told this kind of story, but anyway, he did. Suramya rushed out from the house with the children and suggested we go home immediately.

When I asked her why, she said, 'Didn't you hear what that man [referring to the monk] said? He said that about us. Let us go now.'

After we got home, Suramya started to blame the monk and said that Chitra and some of her friends had laughed at the time. She was really on fire, and watching this, Nandimitra said, 'This is why I said we didn't have to go for that. Why do you think the monk was targeting you? He said it generally to everyone.'

'He was looking at us when he said it,' Suramya replied. 'Sirimath was sitting in front and Chitra's friend laughed and was looking at me.' She then ruled against anyone dealing with Chitra's family going forward. She told me that Kumudu and Sirimath were Facebook friends with Nandana and Nandani and asked me to tell Kumudu and Sirimath to remove them from their account. I asked them to do as their mother said, and Kumudu did so, but Sirimath did not. I understood their pain, becoming friends again and now turning into enemies. This happened previously as well. The irony is that after the death of Dayananda, Suramya wanted to give five thousand dollars to help with the funeral, to which I agreed. Then after the seventh day, she didn't want to have any link with them anymore. I acted as a fool, just to avoid the daily nagging.

In September 2014 Suramya, Kumudu and I again made a visit to Sri Lanka. I asked Kumara, my brother-in-law, to sell our house in Kurunegala and transferred the power of attorney to him. We made a visit to our house in Kurunegala, and it was sad to see how it had been abandoned. However, Kumara couldn't arrange the sale of the house and after speaking with the villager Piyadasa *Mudalali* over the phone, he arranged to sell it to my nephew Mahinda.

In early 2014 Yakalla *Akka* passed away, and three months later that same year, so did Sudu *Akka*. I did not attend the funerals as I had looked after them as much as I could while they were living. More than that, I did not have any money to travel and stay there.

> *Years of fathers' sweats have no place,*
> *compared to mothers' instant tears –*
> *even if they are fake crocodile tears.*
>
> -Nara Somaratne-

Chapter 9

Indicators

By 2015, our three children had grown up and were working. Sirimath had moved to Melbourne. Tirath had two daughters, Lily and Carla, and Kumudu and Sirimath were not yet married. My private superannuation fund matured and I had forty thousand dollars in it. I asked Suramya to keep the amount in a separate bank account for Kumudu's wedding one day. I suggested to Suramya to ask Kumudu whether she would like us to find someone through proposal – to which Kumudu did not agree. In fact, she said, 'If you say it again, I will leave the house.' Later, both Tirath and Sirimath told us not to do it, to let her find a suitable partner herself. We agreed, and it was not mentioned again. By this time, Sirimath was only coming home to Adelaide for holidays. He seemed very busy with his work.

Kumudu had finished her higher studies and was working as a researcher. She and a friend, Eriny, were working in the same discipline. Eriny, her husband Tim and Eriny's parents were lovely people and got to know each other. Each family visited several times for meals and became almost family friends or more likely relatives. When Eriny had a baby girl, Kumudu showed us her photo, first to me and then to Suramya, as I love the little ones. We were all invited to the first birthday party of Eriny and Tim's daughter. There were several guests there, some of whom were introduced to us. Among them was Tim's father and mother. When we returned home, Kumudu said Tim's parents were divorced, but it did not prevent them living like a family. They often joined together for family matters. I was surprised why she talked about divorce at this young age but kept silent.

By this time, I had noticed Kumudu had a habit of telling her friends, especially Eriny, everything that happened at home. I told her it was not a good habit and she should stop it now, as one day when she married, it would create problems for her. Several days later, Suramya started to talk about divorce and said Tim's mother had said that if you have a place to live, the social security benefit is enough to live on, even if you are divorced. I was wondering why she would talk about these things all of a sudden, and I told her I didn't believe it would be possible considering the expenditure we had. How could one possibly live on social security benefits alone? She didn't say anything in return. Meanwhile, she started to work as a volunteer at the Burnside Library. She seemed happy there and made a few friends with some other ladies who were volunteering there too.

By 2016, Suramya started to ignore me more than ever. After work, I would walk from the city, about six kilometres along the Parade, and Suramya would pick me up from there to go home. Most of the time, she would barely talk on the way home. To break the silence, I sometimes asked whether Kumudu was home. Her only answer was either 'no' or 'yes' – there was nothing else to talk about. There were so many things to talk about – her volunteer work, my daily work, but it seemed nothing was happening in our lives. Day by day, I was getting more and more isolated.

Then in 2016, a sad incident happened. Our pet dog, Bella, died due to a complicated heart problem. We did our best keeping her in the veterinarian hospital, but they could not save her. I didn't completely recover from it for several months. At the same time, Suramya started to sleep in a separate bed close to Kumudu's room. When disaster strikes, it seems to come all at once. In 2017, I was diagnosed as having blocked arteries and told I needed a bypass surgery. So, at the end of October, I had triple bypass surgery, and I took one and a half months' leave from the office. Kumudu took a week's leave to attend the hospital with Suramya. After a week, I came home and slowly started to walk and undergo physiotherapy, which Suramya took me to. Most of the day, I spent watching TV – mostly travel documentaries, about Bhutan in particular, as well as some figure skating and the Sri Lankan news. In mid-December 2017, I started to go to work again.

During this time, Tirath's family would come to our home on the weekend, usually for dinner. The girls had a particular attachment to Suramya as she looked after them so Moly could work. Every morning Suramya got ready to go, even on cold winter days. She did this eagerly and with much love. She cooked special foods for the little girls – their favourite was rice and dhal curry. She made little rice balls, which they called 'ricey balls.' It was so nice to see how they enjoy *Aththamma*'s (grandmother's) cooking. One day before they left, Tirath said to me and Suramya, 'It is only the two of you to look after each other.' This seemed strange to me, and we never discussed it again. Maybe I was starting to become angry at anything, since I was living with lots of uncertainty, as there was a plan to replace me at work with a young person. I didn't have financial security for retirement and still Kumudu and Sirimath were not married. Even though we tried selling the house and downsizing, we couldn't sell it. Finally, we decided to sell the house and move to a smaller place, even though it would be below market value. With this in the background, both Suramya and Kumudu were ignoring me at home, which made it a completely unrestful period, and I was becoming more and more angry. There was no one for me to talk at home; I was cornered by my wife and daughter.

I had medical and dental checkups in May and November each year. For dental checkups, I went to Tirath's clinic. It was a pleasure having my dental checkup done by my own son. Tirath is a very pleasant person, and I proudly watched him attending and talking to his other patients. Before my appointment, we would have a coffee at the nearby bakery or in his office kitchen, and have a friendly chat. But in May 2018, he didn't come out to see me, and the practice manager asked whether Tirath knew I was coming. I said 'Yes, he knew, but maybe he's busy.' She said he didn't have any patients that afternoon and she would go and get him. When she came out, she said, 'You can go in now.' Tirath said he was looking for houses for us, but the computer screen showed only the list of his patient's names. The ever-friendly face was not there, and obviously we were not going to have a coffee together.

When I got home, Suramya asked whether Tirath had talked to me. I confirmed that he had, and she exclaimed again, 'Did he talk to you?' Never before had she asked me this, and it seemed a bit strange. I didn't understand, so I kept quiet, not suspecting anybody or anything. Then at my next appointment in November, Tirath again didn't talk to me or even look at me. He just said, 'If you want, you can see the hygienist – your teeth are fine.' When I was done with the hygienist, I asked the practice manager to charge me the full cost just like any other patient, but she did not. I could not imagine what had happened to Tirath.

To add to the confusion, when I went to see the doctor in May 2018, she started shouting at me. Previously, over the last 20 years, she had welcomed me into her clinic. Once again, this added more fuel to my confusion; I was burning with doubt and fear, not knowing what was going on behind the scenes. I told Suramya the doctor shouted at me for no reason, and I did not know why. Her answer was brief: 'She cannot do that to us!' and then she said 'Now you must find a new doctor.' The disrespectful behaviour of the doctor continued for over a year. May 2018 was the most confusing month of my entire life, just like sailing in the middle of the sea without any sense of direction.

In August 2018, my potential replacement from a government department had accepted the offer, and I was to be replaced in January 2019. More and more uncertainty in life began to pop in, and I did not know what to do next. By this time, Suramya and Kumudu had arranged a holiday to Sri Lanka, and they wanted to take Nandimitra and Nelum to a beachside hotel in Galle. I did not want to go with them, but I had agreed to Suramya's request that, while her brother was still alive, we would go and see him. Kumudu was able to partly pay for her trip. By this time, I had no connection with my family members and therefore had not visited any of them. This was more than Suramya's ability to disconnect me from my family; my own negligence played a part as well.

Day by day, Suramya started to make strange comments. One day she said, 'That woman Chitra keeps everything in her mind until the right time and attacks like a snake all at once, not leaving any room to escape.' Then she added, 'Now I know the method.' I asked her why she was saying such things, to which her reply was 'No reason. I just said that.'

After we returned from the holiday, in September we listed the house for sale and began looking for a smaller place to buy. When I was fertilising the garden beds, I injured my shoulder causing broken ligaments and was thereafter unable to do any work; almost everything was done by Kumudu and Suramya. It was a pity to watch them working alone. As part of the preparation for my imminent retirement in January, we went to see the financial planner to discuss and update our financial plan. In the middle of the discussion, Suramya asked whether she was eligible for social security benefits. The surprised financial planner asked, 'Why do you want that when your husband is still working?' Suramya replied, 'I just thought I'd ask in case he loses his job, and I'd like to get a welfare benefit card to go to the movies with my daughter.'

The month of October passed quickly, and we visited various properties available for sale. By this time, I was feeling more and more unrest, as the financial pressure was becoming unbearable. We had practically no saving after working for forty years, and now the house was going to sell below market value. The most unbearable thing was I was abandoned in the house, as both Kumudu and Suramya lived like strangers. It was a vicious cycle: the more they abandoned me, the angrier I became; the more I became angry, the more they abandoned me.

In mid-November, Suramya said she didn't want a special dinner for our thirty-fifth wedding anniversary. I asked her why, and her reply was that this year she would like to have a home-cooked dinner.

I would rather be fooled than fool someone else.

-Nara Somaratne-

Chapter 10

Abandonment

On the afternoon of 28th November, I had a medical appointment with the general practitioner to prepare my annual care plan. In the morning, I went with Suramya to Campbelltown Council to obtain house plans so we could check the sewer pipe system in the house we wanted to purchase. In our previous two houses, we had storm water problems, and we didn't want to deal with that again. We had told the real estate agent that, but the agent did not have the plan, and told us to go to the council and obtain the copies required. When we got to the council, we found that there were no plans, so Suramya and I decided not to buy that house.

However, a second thought came to my mind while I was driving – that we could ask the agent to show us the manhole location, but I didn't tell Suramya. On our way to the agent's office, Suramya got a call from the agent and he asked her whether we had found the plan and were ready to sign the agreement. To which Suramya replied that we were not going to buy that property. I became very angry and scolded Suramya using a filthy word. Suramya was upset and said, 'So that is the way you talk to your wife?' She started to cry. It was completely my fault that I did not tell her my intention. But my anger was not just that incident in isolation; it was the expression of discontent and anger accumulated over months and years which had now just come out through this incident. When we reached the agent's office, it seemed he had already offered the property to the second highest offer. When I came back to the car, I saw Suramya was calling someone and crying. I knew it was Tirath; Suramya could melt her children's heart by crying. She had been using these crying tactics since before our marriage to tell Daya *Aiya* about her troubles with her mother.

On our way home, I asked Suramya what we were going to do next. She didn't reply. I keep saying we do not have much time left to find a house and let us start again from scratch. When I turned the car into our garden, Suramya broke the silence and said, 'Why did you get the heart operation done? You should have died from it.' They had never expected me to survive. However, as soon as we got home, I started looking for properties again and found a possible property for immediate inspection. I told this to Suramya and asked her to come and see whether she liked it.

She replied very sharply: 'I don't want any houses. If needed, only father and daughter can find a house and go.'

I went to the lounge where she was sitting and sat down directly opposite her and asked her what she meant by this.

'I need a separation and I am going to live in a single bedroom unit,' she said.

She then asked me to sign the papers, to which I said angrily, 'I will sign a thousand times.' I thought she said it because of her anger and there was no real meaning to it. She continued to talk angrily: 'I went to see a psychologist as you told me I have no brain, and the children know about it. Our doctor found me the psychologist to consult.' My quick answer was, 'I never said that at all. What I said was whatever you do no one knows, as you play your cards underhand.' This was the reason Tirath had ignored me and the doctor had shouted at me. This itself proved how underhanded she was; at home she prepared me tea, and washed my cup and plate, even talking lovingly in front of others.

As it was almost time for my doctor's appointment, I hurried to get there. It took nearly an hour to finish the care plan and medical check-up. As soon as I came out of the clinic, I received a text message from Suramya saying Tirath had come to take her to his place, and she would never come back. It confirmed that it was Tirath she was talking to over the phone at the agent's office earlier. When I got home, I found that some of the cupboards were open and clothes had been taken away. In the evening, Kumudu came home after work. Her eyes were swollen from crying. She went to her room and changed. I asked her to have dinner, whatever we had available. After dinner, she told me she had come to get her clothes, and she was going to live with her mother. I didn't say anything, as it was fair enough. Poor children also take on the burden and stupidity of their parents. For the next few days, Kumudu came home to Wattle Park to see me, which was very kind of her.

On 29th November, I went to the office in the morning and had a coffee with Glenn. I told him Suramya had left and was staying with Tirath and saying she wanted a separation. He asked what had happened, and I told him about the incident and how common these things were, but how usually everything would become normal within a day. I told him the pain was a thousand times worse than the loss of Bella, and tears fell on the coffee table. Later in the evening, I received a text message from Sirimath, who was living in Melbourne, asking me to ring him when I was ready.

He understood my state of mind. I texted him back saying I would ring him in a day or two. On Saturday morning, I telephoned Suramya and told her to come back home without any further joking around. I asked her to think about not just our lives, but to think about our daughter and granddaughters as well. To this she replied that she was wondering whether Tirath would become angry if she came back. Did this mean Tirath had influenced her? I said, 'Then ask the children before you make your decision.' Later in the day, I received a text message that she wouldn't be coming back.

On the following Sunday morning, I telephoned Sirimath. It was a brief conversation. He said that *Amma* had gone to see a lawyer about a separation and that '*Achchi*, you too should also find a lawyer to protect your interest.' Not knowing anything much about separation and divorce procedure, I said, 'It would be 50% each wouldn't it?'

'It may not be the case *Achchi*, you may still need a lawyer,' said Sirimath. Through an internet search, I learned a bit more about separation and divorce procedures and found a solicitor close to my office.

December arrived, and it was the Christmas holidays. Sirimath came home and stayed with me at the Wattle Park house, though he went to see his brother and sister. By this time, Kumudu and Suramya had found a temporary place to live until they could buy or rent a house. After Sirimath returned to Melbourne, I started to feel lonely, initially after dark with the quietness, but then it gradually spread throughout the day. To avoid it, I went to West Beach several times and for a drive to see where we had lived in Hackham, to Colonnades, the shopping centre in Noarlunga, and Tirath's kindergarten. Nothing helped – as soon as I came home, loneliness started to strike again. There was no one to talk to and everyone close to me had left.

> *Many people have come and left, and it has been always good because they emptied some space for better people. It is a strange experience, that those who have left me have always left places for a better quality of people. I have never been a loser.*
>
> -OSHO-

Chapter 11

Recovery and gaining happiness

On the advice of Sarath, I attended a three-day meditation session in mid-January and met some other community members who also participated. From the first day onwards, I felt myself becoming relaxed. At the end of the third day, most of my stress had gone, and I started to meditate at home in the morning and late in the evening before going to bed. I noticed my daily work at home and in the office become normal. I wanted to continue meditation practice and went to see what programs were available at Buddha House, a Tibetan Buddhist Centre in Magill. What a surprise – the secretary told me there was a three-day Dhamma talk and meditation with a visiting Tibetan monk starting the next day on how to turn misery to happiness. I attended and, in a nutshell, it was simply about letting go and freeing oneself. If you hold on to anything or any relationships, you are caught and it will in the end bring misery. Thereafter, I attended regular meditation sessions on Sundays.

Miracle after miracle started to happen. I was not angry anymore; even if someone abused me, I did not become angry. I started to look at it as merely a passing sound-wave through my ears. Glenn helped me to recover and advised me to visit my friends in Brisbane. The chosen replacement for my position had got a permanent position in his department and declined to accept the position, so I could continue working in the same job. The loneliness started to disappear. I do not know whether it was a result of the meditation or healing with time. Maybe both. Instead of loneliness, now aloneness started appearing.

Meantime, our house had sold, and the agent informed me settlement was planned for the end of February 2019. I found a two-bedroom unit in nearby Kensington Park and Glenn helped me to shift my furniture. Without him, I could not do anything as my shoulder injury was causing severe pain. Glenn had dramatically changed my life. He was always helping me – he was my friend, sometimes like a father, sometimes like a brother.

In March, I visited the east coast – Brisbane and Sydney. In Sydney, I met with Gamini and Ranjith and visited Chitra *Akka* who was living with her daughter Nandani. Chitra *Akka* and my younger sister Kumari were good friends, and I knew she would pass the message to her. I told everyone what happened and Chitra *Akka* said she would tell this to Kumari. After meeting friends in Brisbane and thanking them for their help and guidance, I went to Palm Cove to have a relaxing time alone. Here again, I continued to do my meditation in the morning and evening and visited the Great Barrier Reef, which was like a dream come true. After coming back to Adelaide, I went to Melbourne to attend the forty-fifth batch get together. Batch mates from all over the world arrived; some of them I had not seen for the last forty years. One thing became evident, that almost everyone knew about what had happened to me and my marriage break-up. There was one special person, Piya who came from Canada, who talked to me at length. He was one of my close friends when we were in high school as well as at university. After going back to Canada, he sent me a moving email:

My dear Senevi,

I came to Canada/Calgary on 14 (March 2019). I was very happy that I met you after long time. I thought about you before coming to Melbourne.

I hope you got lot of information/advice from other friends; therefore, I do not like to repeat again and again. But I have to say something, I know you long-long time, please bear with me.

I know you from school, we were good friends. You always work hard, never give up, punctual, not blamed to others. You are not the best in the class, but your achievements no one can challenge in our class at Matale. I am sure you have done 110% to your children and wife, that is a good *karma*. I know it is difficult to detach from everything, but reality is that. Ask the question from yourself, what should I do now. Remember, if you can detach from your past then you will hurt only one time. Do not think about the past, do not blame anyone including you or your wife, just think about tomorrow, think about you, your meals, your exercise, your health, your happiness, good things you did and then you do some meditation. Get rid of negative thoughts, be positive always, love to yourself and try to enjoy yourself. You are a good cook, make good meals for you, go to the office, and talk with office staff smiley face every day, enjoy their company, do some positive works, mentor juniors to do some good works and enjoy at work.

Remember you work hard and achieved so many things, help lot to your children to grow as a good human. Same way from today develops your life, mentally and physically that is the challenge in your hand today, you can do it, trust yourself. You remember that you did some works nicely some years ago, how you did it, what are the achievements. Same attitudes/principles apply for you now.

Try to listen to Ajan Braham dharma talks, any others you like and practise two types of meditations every day, start with 15-min, you are alone now, no one disturb you, this will clean up your mind.

Eat well, dress nicely, talk to your friends in Australia, travel some places you never visited, do something for yourself. If you can come and visit us.

If possible, go for the meditation retreats, Western Australia Ajan Braham temple. Now I asked you to do so many things, just think what you can do, **if you can do one or two, that will be good enough. However, Most importantly Love Yourself, Treat Your Self Nicely, Go for Long Walks.**

Regards,
Piya

Following this, I listened to Ajan Braham's discourses, with particular interest in the Letting Go discourse. In addition, some of the more frequently listened to non-dual Vedantic discourses were from Swami Sarvapriyananda, Swami Tadatmananda, the Who Am I inquiry of Ramana Maharshi, David Godman, Mooji, the profound talks of Jiddu Krishnamurthi, Rupert Spira, Jason Gregory and Allan Watts.

During the easter holiday in April, I went to Darwin and visited Kakadu and Lichfield national parks and Katherine Gorge. This was a very relaxing time. In addition, I visited Broome with interest to see the Horizontal Falls and Staircase to the Moon. By this time,

Chitra *Akka* had telephoned Kumari *Nangi* and told her the story. She telephoned me and said that I wasn't alone; they were all there with me even though I had not seen them for years. According to her, everyone had cried upon hearing the news, including the villager Piyadasa *Mudalali*. Kumari *Nangi* told me that she would visit me in June.

While in the rented unit, I found an independent retirement unit in Magill. Glenn came to see the unit and went through the contract documents. He was happy about the unit and the contractual arrangement. In mid-May, I shifted to the retirement village; once again Glenn and his son-in-law came to shift the furniture. Nandana telephoned and told me he could come with some friends to shift furniture, but by that time, Glenn had already arranged it. Sometimes I would sit on a chair inside the house or a bench outside the unit or go to a park and sit on a bench alone, observing thought flow. There were instances where I experienced no thoughts, only the complete silence of the mind. This is what Jiddu Krishnamurthi talked about in meditation. Even though it last only a few seconds, it brought happiness and bliss.

In the middle of June, my sister arrived and stayed with me in the village. During this time, I had to undergo prostate surgery, and only Moly visited the hospital with Lily and Carla. Jeff was in town, and he came to take me back to the unit after I was discharged from the hospital. Unable to tolerate the winter, my sister became ill in July and went to Sydney to stay with Chitra *Akka* and Nandani. They took care of her up until her departure to Sri Lanka. In October 2019, I underwent eye surgery to remove cataracts in both eyes. This time I had no help from anyone. At the end of December to mid-January 2020, I visited Laos, Sri Lanka and Oman to refresh my memories and see old friends. A travel restriction was imposed in 2020 due to the spread of COVID-19, which was lifted in 2022. This enabled me to travel to my dream country Bhutan, followed by tours of Tasmania and New Zealand. In July 2023, I went to Sri Lanka and met all the relatives once again. With my sister Kumari, we organised a family-get-together tour to Jaffna, bringing together all family members. Everyone enjoyed it, and now they are closer than ever. In addition, in mid-July I completed a Scandinavian tour of Finland, Sweden, Norway and Denmark. Whenever possible I hope to see more and more countries travelling throughout the world. Travelling to see the world is a childhood dream of mine.

Wherever I travel, my daily meditation practices continue. There are three main religious philosophies that I follow:

Buddhism: Emptiness (*Sunyata*) – there is no independent existence. It is a mode of perception, a way of looking at experience. It adds nothing to and takes nothing away from the raw data of physical and mental events. We are one with the universe.

Non-dual Vedanta – particularly the Ashtavakra Gita: We are attached to no one, and no one is attached to us, because I am pure consciousness. For pure consciousness, there is nothing to add and nothing to take away. The fourth verse of the Four Ways to Dissolution states that:

You are perfect, changeless,
Through misery and happiness,
Hope and despair,
Life and death.
This is the state of dissolution.

Taoism: Effortless action (*Wu Wei*) is the basis for philosophy of flow – let the life flow like a river, letting go without holding to anything. Those who flow as life flows know they need no other force. Live harmoniously with the natural environment with three principals to follow: humility, compassion and simplicity – by letting go of ego with minimum resistance. Everything is connected and we are part of a greater whole.

Overall, I have nothing to regret. I have gone through misery and happiness, hope and despair many times. What I had was a rare opportunity to experience all of them in one life cycle. I looked after my mother and siblings, helping as much as I could; I contributed to my profession developing new approaches in groundwater science; raised a family doing the maximum as a husband and a father providing comfortable living with food and nourishment, educating the children, providing protection and discipling whenever it was needed.

Going back through life from childhood to now, there are few things I should not have done. I cannot go back and correct them as it is impossible. I do not regret them, as they were the best solutions at the time. For certain, I have not seen anger since November 2018 and am not likely to become angry again. I am happy and will live that way for the next few years, until I merge with the greater consciousness.

Fear

It is said that before entering the sea,
a river trembles with fear.

She looks back at the path she has travelled,
from the peaks of the mountains, the long winding
road crossing forests and villages.

And in front of her, she sees an ocean so vast, that to enter
seems nothing more than to disappear for ever.

But there is no other way.

The river cannot go back.

Nobody can go back.

To go back is impossible in existence.

The river needs to take the risk of entering the ocean,
because only then will fear disappear,

Because that's where the river will know

It's not about disappearing into the ocean, but of
becoming the ocean.

-Khalil Gibran-

Chapter 12

Manifestation of Karma

Some people have the view that anything that manifests in life is not because of *karma* in this life or a previous one. However, I believe there is some truth that *karma* is a strong factor, and in fact one of the most important laws governing our lives. *Karma* is just a law of nature, the law of cause and effect on the psychophysical plane. According to Buddhism, the term *karma* specifically refers to volition – the intention or motive behind an action. The law of *karma* can be understood on two levels, which indicates the vast scope of its implications in our lives. On one level, *karma* refers to the experience of cause and effect over a period. We perform an action, and sometime later we begin to experience its results. On the other level, *karma* has to do with quality of mind in the very moment of action. When we experience the mind state of love, there comes naturally, along with it, a feeling of openness and love that is its immediate fruit. Similarly, when there are moments of greed or hatred, in addition to whatever future results will come, we also experience the painful energies that arise with those states. Our direct awareness of how the *karmic* law is working in each moment can be a strong motivation to develop skillful states of mind that create happiness for us in the moment, as well as producing the fruit of well-being in the future.

Going back to my own life, after visiting Suramya's house for the first time in 1983, we came back to Polonnaruwa via Kurunegala. Gune was driving the car, and no one talked for a while. The road was full of traffic. Deepa broke the silence, saying, 'How was she Senevi?' I did not reply, continuing to look out the window at roadside vendors in small towns and passing paddy fields. Karu started to joke and tease: 'Maybe Senevi is thinking about her …' and this teasing went on all the way. Gune was less talkative, but made a few naughty jokes. I managed to respond without saying yes or no, but told them I had to think about it, and that I was not in a hurry to marry as I still had an elder and younger sister to marry before I thought of myself.

'Fair enough. We have time to find you a girl,' Karu said. We stopped for a cup of tea at our house in Mallawapitiya. I introduced my friends to my mother, elder sister Punchi *Akka* and younger sister Kumari *Nangi*. Kumari *Nangi* was enthralled hearing that I went to see a girl in Kandy who was a school friend of Deepa. She asked more about her, the place and whereabouts, as she knew the Peradeniya area as she had lived there during her university days. I told her she was from Udahagama along the Kandy–Colombo Road, a short distance from Peradeniya town. The house was by the roadside and on a small hillock. Kumari *Nangi* exclaimed with surprise, saying, 'Oh, I know that place! It is almost next door to Ramani's elder sister's house. Ramani was her batchmate and best friend. She asked whether I liked her, and Deepa answered: 'He never said anything.'

'It is one of the items on my list of considerations,' I said.

On our way back to Pollonnaruwa, Deepa told me I had a lovely, friendly younger sister and asked what she was doing and whether she had any boyfriend to marry.

'She is working in a government corporation and has no boyfriend; we are looking for a nice young man,' I said.

Deepa, being talkative, started again and said, 'We will find her a boy from Kandy.' Then Karu said, 'It is a good deal – you give one to Kandy and take one from Kandy.' Gune said his wife Daya's younger brother was also a graduate teacher and was looking for a good girl.

'I am going to propose her to him,' he said. 'I am serious. He is also a government contractor with good earnings and is building a house in Anuradhapura.'

Deepa said jokingly, 'If this works, I am going to resign from teaching and do full-time match-making charging ten per cent of the dowry.'

When we reached Melsiripura, we stopped to buy arracks to take with us. The tavern was famous for selling unmixed arrack and three of us bought two bottles each. We were hungry so Gune suggested we stop at Dambulla rest-house for dinner. We were supposed to go to Suramya's place for lunch but missed it because we had had two tyre punctures on our way, and it took a long time to find a place to repair the tyres. At Dambulla, we had dinner and started the rest of our journey to Polonnaruwa. Karu and Deepa quickly fell asleep in the back seat. I had a chat with Gune on various matters other than matrimony.

The following morning, Nissanka and Keerthi, who shared the house with me, asked about the trip at the breakfast table. We were busy with our daily work and on weekends, I went home to see my mother. Two weeks after our trip to Kandy, I met Karu and Deepa at their quarters. We would usually meet friends in small groups and share jokes and various stories. Karu and Deepa asked whether I had decided, and I said 'Not yet.' Then they both said they wanted to tell you something – that she had had a love affair with her cousin, the younger brother of Chitra, Dayananda's wife, and his name was Wickrama. And they added they didn't know how far it has gone. Karu said it might be a typical school-time love affair – almost all girls and boys had this kind of love affair during their school days. He suggested this may well be a similar case, and may not necessarily have been a serious affair. That's when I told them to let her know I had no interest in her. Deepa said she would either write to Suramya or tell her mother to pass on the message whenever she next telephoned home. Thereafter, we never talked about it and both Karu and Deepa asked me to stay for dinner, and I was obliged.

A few days later, I met both Karu and Deepa again in a social gathering of engineers in the area. Deepa said she had passed the message to her mother, and she would contact Suramya's house. I said I was going home and planned to go to Kandy to meet a couple of friends. They both asked me to visit Deepa's mother, as she had some good news about two prospective marriage proposals.

'Well,' I said, 'whether there is any proposal or not, I will visit your parents to see how they are doing.'

As promised, I visited Deepa's house. As I parked the car, I saw the door was closed and someone was sitting on the veranda. I approached the house and recognised her – it was Suramya with a little girl. I inquired whether anyone was at home and Suramya replied that aunty had gone to a nearby shop and would return soon. She has asked the people who rented their annex. I stayed for a few minutes and had a little chat with the little girl, who was maybe ten or twelve years old. I asked her name, and in reply she said 'Sugandhika Udahagama.' Then I asked her about school, which grade she was in, about her hobbies and so on, just to pass the time. Suramya said Sugandhika was her second elder brother's daughter. I wanted to tell Suramya that I did not have any more interest in her but thought it was very impolite. In addition, if Deepa's mother had already conveyed the message, it was very embarrassing.

As it had already taken more than ten minutes, I thought of leaving and at the very moment of that thought, Deepa's mother appeared in the driveway with a vegetable basket in her hand. While opening the front door, Deepa's mother apologised that she had not been at home when I arrived. She invited us to the lounge room and showed me a chair. Suramya called her aunty, as they had known each other for a long time. To start with the talk, I said both Karu and Deepa are doing well there, and I might have to go soon as I had to visit a few more friends. Deepa's mother insisted on me staying for lunch, as it was already past midday. She said uncle had gone to the town and he would be late so we should have lunch. As she started to arrange the table, Suramya joined her, passing out the table mats, serviettes and bringing out dishes. While doing so, she said to Deepa's mother, 'We have to buy an umbrella for Deepa.'

Buying an umbrella for a person who arranges marriage literally means that the proposal was successful. As a habit, matchmakers in Sri Lanka get an umbrella among other gifts and payments. A typical matchmaker walks from village to village looking for prospective brides and grooms, carrying an umbrella. At the very moment Suramya said this, a thought crossed my mind that this girl is thinking of me, and I should not frustrate her; this may be my destiny. This is the moment my previous *karma* linked into this life.

Soon after lunch, Suramya left, and I had a little chat with Deepa's mother. She said that Deepa had telephoned and informed her she should convey to Suramya's house the news that I did not want to go ahead with the proposal, but so far, she had not had time to do so.

'Well,' she said, 'now that you have both met accidentally, there's no need to tell them that.' She continued on to say that Suramya was a good girl and a good housekeeper. After a short while, I left the house. On arriving back at Polonnaruwa, both Karu and Deepa were surprised to hear what had happened. Karu joked, 'If you have to pay your past *karma*, no matter how and what, it comes after you and gets you.' We all laughed.

> *Karma is the result of our actions. Our good and bad Karmas follow us wherever we are; we cannot get away from them even if we want. Karma follows us everywhere, in this life and the next, just like wheels of a cart follow the bull.*
>
> -Dhammapadaya-

Forthcoming publication, a short story on:

Siver Bangles and Gold Bangles

Nara Somaratne